Praise from the jud

From Christopher Brookmyre and Marissa Haetzman, Edinburgh Short Story Award 2024.

On the winning story, *The Coffin Path* by Kerry Andrew.

> *We loved not merely the language and imagery, but the rhythm of its flow... A haunting, tragic and yet optimistic piece of storytelling that conveyed a lifetime, but also a future.*

On *Space enough for you* by Sabrina Wolfe, second prize.

> *It was suffused with a pervasive sense of a world ever reducing and the claustrophobic awareness of another person's anger...*

On *Wing Mirrors* by Frances McKendrick, winner of the Isobel Lodge Award 2024 for the top story by an unpublished writer living in Scotland.

> *The emotion felt painfully authentic... An evocative piece of writing that brought home the agonizing complexity of parental love and responsibility.*

From Zoë Strachan and Louise Welsh, Edinburgh Flash Fiction Award 2024.

On the winning story, *What You Do When You Find Your Mother Dead* by Hannah Retallick.

> *The story has a rhythm that suggests panic... There is so much intimacy, line by line.. it builds and builds...*

The Edinburgh Anthologies
Volume One

The Outlier

and other stories

Edited by
Sara Cameron McBean
and Claire Rocha

Scottish Arts Trust
www.scottishartstrust.org

The Edinburgh Anthologies
Volume One

The Outlier

and other stories

Edited by
Sara Cameron McBean
and Claire Rocha

Scottish Arts Trust
www.scottishartstrust.org

Other publications from the Scottish Arts Trust

The Desperation Game and other stories from the Scottish Arts Trust Story Awards 2014-2018 (Volume 1). Edited by Sara Cameron McBean and Hilary Munro (2019)

Life on the Margins and other stories from the Scottish Arts Trust Story Awards 2019-2020 (Volume 2). Edited by Sara Cameron McBean and Michael Hamish Glen (2020)

A Meal for the Man in Tails and other stories from the Scottish Arts Club Story Awards 2021 (Volume 3). Edited by Sara Cameron McBean and Michael Hamish Glen (2021)

Beached and other stories from the Scottish Arts Club Story Awards 2022 (Volume 4). Edited by Sara Cameron McBean and Claire Rocha (2022)

Solemates and other stories from the Scottish Arts Club Story Awards 2023 (Volume 5). Edited by Sara Cameron McBean and Claire Rocha (2023)

Rosalka: The Silkie Woman and other stories, plays and poems by Isobel Lodge (2018)

Edinburgh Writing Awards

scottishartstrust.org/writing

Edinburgh Short Story Award

First prize £3,000: Open to writers worldwide and stories on any topic up to 2,000 words. Enter from 1 October to 28 February annually.

> The Isobel Lodge Award (£750) for top short story entered by an unpublished writer living in Scotland.

> The Write Mango Award (£300) for the most amusing, bizarre story.

> The First Write Award (£300) for the top story by an unpublished writer, worldwide.

Edinburgh Flash Fiction Award

First prize £2,000: Open to writers worldwide and stories on any topic up to 250 words. Enter from 1 May to 31 August annually.

> The Golden Hare Award (£500) is for the top flash fiction entry by a writer living in Scotland, published or unpublished.

> The Write Mango Flash Award (£300) for the most amusing, bizarre story.

Authors of at least 20 leading entries from the short story and flash fiction competitions are offered publication in our next anthology.

Edinburgh True Flash Award

First prize £500: For writers worldwide and creative non-fiction, memoirs, auto-fiction up to 250 words. Enter from 1 May to 31 August annually.

Edinburgh Young Adult Novel Award

First prize £1,500: For writers worldwide and novels or graphic novels suitable for readers age 12 and older. Enter from 1 October to 28 February annually.

Edinburgh Essay Award

First prize £1,000: For writers worldwide and essays on any topic up to 2,000 words. Enter from 1 October to 28 February annually.

Authors of the top fifteen entries are offered publication The Edinburgh Essays, our new journal of inspired non-fiction.

Contents

The Coffin Path

(A Lyke Wake Dirge)

by Kerry Andrew

First Prize, Edinburgh Short Story Award 2024

One step, then another, then another.

The heather is almost black. Cold that burns under the skin.

One step, then another, then another. We shift him on our shoulders, our breath in clouds, complaints now wordless. By the glassy light of a wolf moon, the three of us carry our load over the moor.

Just like him to die in January, the bitter month, the biting month. The month of darkness beyond cheer.

'Can we stop?'

'You just asked that.'

'Because I need to. My back's half-broke.'

'We'll get to the brow of that hill, like we said.'

'It's too far.'

'Come on. You're as hard as ironstone.'

'Right now, I'm as hard as soup.'

Brittle moor. Hurting moor. With its music of wind and lapwing and our hungry stomachs. Our home, for better or worse. Mostly worse.

'He said we weren't to stop. We'll do it right.'

'But he's dead.'

'The brow of that hill.'

Three sisters, a year apart in age so that our mother, when she was alive, looked at us with despair as well as love. Joan, Alice, Edith.

'You're not the one carrying extra.'

'You're in the middle. We're bearing more.'

'Is this what we're going to be like? Now that he's gone?'

'No. Just for this bit.'

'Shall we sing again?'

> *This ae nighte, this ae nighte,*
> *Every nighte and alle,*
> *Fire and fleet and candle-lighte,*
> *And Christe receive thy saule.*

The lawyer sat with us the day after we'd found him, swollen on the scullery's slate floor, his heart burst and spreading into his body. 'There is a will,' the scarlet-nosed lawyer had said. 'But... well.' We'd looked at one another.

Under the mothering moon we walk. She left us, our mother, when Joan was no higher than her thigh. After that, Joan would point to the moon at its fullest and say 'there she is', her face as pale and bruised as it had been in life. 'But where's the rest of her?' Edith would say. 'Under the blanket,' Alice would say, once she was old enough to share the lie.

In truth, she lay under a blanket of cold earth, three fields up. A lumpen sandstone, scratched crudely. *Lol Walker. Wife and mother.*

Three brides. Each performing the duties of a wife. All duties, you understand.

'My daughters Joan, Alice and Edith Walker must carry me over the coffin path to my burial place at the parish church,' the lawyer had read. 'No horse, no cart. No other hands. They must not rest until it is done. Then my house and lands are theirs.' The lawyer lowered the paper and gazed over his coin-sized spectacles. 'It is an unusual request, but I'm afraid –'

'There are ghosts on that path,' whispered Edith.

'We'll do it,' Joan said.

Higher. The moor rises, the sky lowers, and here is the stinging magic of snow. The heather made bridesmaid.

'At least we can see better,' says Alice.

We have walked over the moor for one day, and there is at least another to come.

He did not think we would do it. Did not think we *could* do it.

When we first picked up the coffin, we could not get him above our propped knees. Any higher, and Alice fell on her arse and laughed. 'It's impossible. We need a fucking shire horse.'

'We're doing it,' said Edith, though she was by now five months with child.

Again we tried, and again, until somehow he was on Joan's right shoulder, and Alice's left, with Edith in the middle.

'Now what?' said Alice.

'Now we take one step,' said Joan. 'And another. Shall we sing?'

And afterlong we went.

He liked to hear us. 'Better you sing than your jangling,' he'd say, and nod, and our three voices would thread

together – Edith highest, then Alice, then Joan. We'd learn a
tune and then knit our notes around it, so that it grew,
widened. He would hum, a short, low sound, and watch
the fire.

A big man, Abraham Walker. A monolith atop Cold Moor.
Broad, too, with hands like anvils. We knew the strength in
them as well as any Bible story.

Don't think we haven't noticed the irony. Our family name
being Walker and us slipshod and blistered.

'He wants to kill us,' says Alice. 'He always did.'

'But he won't,' says Joan.

The lawyer saw us off from the house. Scratched a note in
ink and pen on calfskin. Looked guilty.

Cold Moor. Hasty Bank. Smuggler's Trod and Esklets.
South Flat How. White Cross and Shunner Howe.

'This is his curse,' Alice says.

Their father, yoked on their shoulders, turning them into
panting, hopeless beasts.

'Not for long,' says Joan.

Each of us wore his marks, as our mother had.

'This is burnt,' he'd say, looking at some black-edged
mutton that Edith had lifted her eyes from for one moment
while dreaming.

'This is filthy,' he'd say about the scullery, because Alice
had overlooked some strands of straw on the stone.

'This is damp,' he'd say, hand on the bedsheet, that Joan
had gathered in on smell of rain.

Wormy fruit in the apple-cradle. Mice in the ambry. All of it their doing.

The rainbow children, went the whispers at church, because one girl's bruises would be yellowing as another purpled.

Coffin path. Corpse Road. Bier Road. Lyke Way. Lych Way. The path on which to carry the dead from remote dwelling to mother church. A soul's last journey.

'We are born to die,' he would say, in the slow hours after dinner. 'Doesn't matter what happens in between. It's forgotten.'

Not to us.

Crows and silver birches. Gorse and pine. The last breath of ancient forest. More than once, we slip in the bogs, the coffin tipping, but our father ordered his coffin well-tied, as if he knew we'd fall. We are sure we will never be dry again.

A golden plover gives a lonely, piping call. Odd, for it to be so high on the moor in winter.

'Ghosts,' says Edith, her teeth chattering. 'There are ghosts.' She steps out from the coffin and crouches in a ball, her arms over her ears, curled around her plum-shaped belly.

And there are, moving almost soundlessly across the moor, souls that have flittered loose from their coffins on their last journey.

But then we hear the scutting of their teeth, and a call like an old drunk, and feel relief. Twinters, nothing more.

'Edith, it's all right,' says Alice.

'Just sheep,' says Joan. 'Not ghosts.'

Abbeys bought this land and turned it over to grazing, leaving only shadow-woods. Our mother would tell us the names like a lullaby. Oak and ash and willow. Herb-paris and yellow archangel. Violet crown cup.

The old king may have broken the abbeys now, but the sheep remain. Maybe they are ghosts, after all. Ghosts amongst ghosts.

'Is it Frank's?' Joan would whisper.

'Is it Joseph's?' Alice would whisper.

Edith would simply put her head down and carry on sweeping.

Her sisters could not fathom why Abraham did not seek the young man out, pummel him until he was bog-coloured. Instead, though he did not touch her belly, he still hit her.

'You'll never leave this place,' he said once. 'This house, this hill, is in your bones. You will reap and sow and suffer all the hardship that I have, and my father before me.'

Blue man in-th'-Moss. Wheeldale Stepping Stones. Fen Bogs. Eller Beck. Lilla Howe.

The coffin digs. There are welts on our necks. Bruises on our shoulders. Lower backs feeling splintered. We do not wait for coffin-rests, but take it in turns to sit in the mire and weep.

'I think I can smell it. The sea.'

Salt as grain, as dream. Joan and Alice wonder quietly if Edith's mind is untethering in her exhaustion.

'We're not there yet,' says Joan.

'But soon,' says Alice.

He hated the sea, did Abraham Walker. Never even set foot on sand. Wouldn't eat fish that weren't from a river or pond. 'A grave, nothing more,' he'd say. 'A watery hell.' Someone once told them at church that his cherished uncle, the man who'd carried him about on his shoulders, had been a fisherman, and drowned, and that Abraham had screamed and sweated nightmares for months.

At twilight, the great church tower widens into view. None of us have seen it since we were small.

Not even our mother is buried here.

Along with two gravediggers, the lawyer is waiting. He even looks at his timepiece. 'Ah,' he says.

Edith collapses, white-faced. Her fingers are blue.

'I should have thought to have a man accompany you,' he says, doubtfully. 'In order to –'

Alice stalks up to him, rips off her boot, sticks her bloodied bare heel under his nose. 'You think this is a falsehood?' Rips off her other boot.

He recoils. 'Well, no, I –'

'We have done as he bid,' says Joan.

'Water,' says Edith. 'Please.'

A godly man. Hypocrites often are. Reading from the Bible as if it were more important than milking, or harvest. Eyeing with relish the life after this one. 'When I am in my grave, all will be right between me and our Lord,' he'd say. 'I look forward to meeting him.'

After we have recovered ourselves enough, the parish priest comes over, his cowl flapping like a cormorant's wings. We barely hear his words, minds and bodies dumb

19

with pain. The coffin is lowered into the pocket of earth. No one sings.

The gravediggers pick up their spades.

'We'll do it ourselves,' says Joan.

'But the men –' says the lawyer.

'No. You can all go home. We've come this far. We'll see it through.'

The lawyer nods, and scratches on calfskin with pen and ink.

We wait until they have all gone. Wait longer. Look at each other.

Together, we three use the ropes to haul out the coffin. Alice has to go in and get her arms underneath it.

Together, we three pile the earth into the grave. Pat it down.

Together, soil-stained, moor-stained, we three look at the coffin.

We lean down, heave the coffin onto our shoulders again, and walk.

Each daughter thought he only sought us alone on moonless nights, long ago. None of us knew about the other until his blood was cold. Two of us didn't know that it had continued longer, into her monthly bleedings, with Edith.

Not so far now. The moor has become a mattress. Our legs light as a heron's. Our swollen, raw feet do not give us moan. We walk on, towards the sea-light.

Jugger Howe Ravine. Stony Marl Moor. Smuggler's Rock.

Ravenscar.

'It's beautiful,' says Alice.

Winter water is a baying animal. It roars, cave and hollow, rock and wave. It turns and snarls and beckons. *Come.*

The cliffs are black here, and saw-toothed. A high tide.

'Now?' says Edith.

'Now,' says Joan.

Together, we heft him from our shoulders.

The will did not say that he should be buried at the church. Just brought there.

The coffin cracks against the cliffside but does not break. It tumbles, hits the water. Is lightly battered against the rocks. Falters. Sinks. Wood and body smothered by salt.

No gravestone. No shadow of church tower.

'This one won't be like him,' Edith says, one hand on her belly.

'They won't,' say Alice and Joan, together.

On the horizon, the dawn thickens like cream-top milk.

We travel back across the moor in a cart, to the house we hate. We will sell it and live by the sea. It howls as much as the hills, but there are people, warm fires, and smoked fish. Music that summons light, not darkness.

We will bring up the child, and he will be a hale and smiling boy and then sturdy young man, as sweet as clover honey, who always gives thanks for his three, ox-strong, always-singing mothers.

What You Do When You Find Your Mother Dead

by Hannah Retallick

Winner, Edinburgh Flash Fiction Award 2024

Remember that you haven't removed your shoes. Teeter between the shoe rack and her body slumped across the sofa. Tiptoe across the plushy cream carpet. Check for certain, fingers on her neck. Feel your own throbbing pulse in her tangled red curls. You're so alive, painfully alive, and she's. Room temperature. You've forgotten something. Is it your school bag? No, that's cutting your shoulder, heavy with what you should know. Inform the next of kin. You, her only daughter, need to be informed immediately. You inform yourself but don't believe it because you're only twelve and she was only forty and perfectly healthy. Perhaps you should inform the next-of next of kin, Uncle Ted, and he can inform you back, break it to you more gently. What were you going to say to her before? Words had hung from your lips as you stomped in, forgetting to remove your shoes. Homework. A question about tectonic shifts, something you couldn't understand. Ground shifting beneath us, the most terrifying thing you could imagine until... 3:37 pm. Yes, you check on your phone, like it might matter. Sit. Sit before you fall. Let the bag tip from your shoulder. Feel the blood surge back into your arm. Grasp your phone, all you have, and search for a number you've never needed. Google what to do when you find your mother dead, because no one ever told you, did they. They didn't think it was any of your business.

Space enough for you

by Sabrina Wolfe

Second Prize, Edinburgh Short Story Award 2024

You are sitting at the formica table in the kitchen, cutting an apple, looking out of the window. The willow tree catches your eye, as it always does. The branches hang over the pavement, brushing the heads of anyone walking past. You eat the apple and wait for something to happen. For someone to arrive. You are fed up of watching everything from behind a pane of glass.

You are old. You are 83. You are an age you never imagined you could reach, and yet. Here it is.

You are dressed in black. An elegant, loose dress that you bought in Paris, many years ago, from the boutique by your apartment. This morning, you chose a bangle from your collection. It is pink. Plastic. A chunky octagon. It knocks against your wrist. Every day you wear black clothes with one bright accessory. After choosing the bangle, you painted your lips to match. Your lipstick collection is extensive. You used a magnifying mirror to draw the liner carefully, taking care that the colour didn't bleed to the wrinkles around your mouth.

You spoke to your reflection when you were finished. There, you said, there. And you brushed your hair, which is white not silver, still thick, and reaches to your shoulders. You counted to one hundred as you brushed.

Now, you are sitting in the kitchen of your townhouse in Notting Hill. You have lived here since you were first married. But it has been only you for 20 years now. It is only you, and all of your furniture, living together on the ground floor. Your son – his name is David – converted the house into three flats, and you rent out the top two floors. The furniture moved downstairs when you did. David tells you there is not enough space for you and all of it, on this single floor. David tells you that often, he tells you that at least once a week.

You are scared of your son, sometimes, though you don't know why and you don't like to fully think about it.

The dishwasher is running in the flat of the family above you. Their washing machine is at the end of a spin cycle. The ceiling above your head vibrates. There will be low water pressure in your flat. You must wait until later to wash up.

You sit and listen to the noises coming from the house above you, the house that used to be yours and now creaks to other people's movements. You feel alone in your kitchen. Alone in your flat.

You listen to the noises, and you think of your friend, Delphine (who was not ever really your friend) but find you can only think of her in fragments. The way the sunlight fell through the open balcony onto the herringbone floor of the Paris apartment. Freshly washed white sheets, an immovable lipstick stain on the corner of one pillowcase. The smell of Guerlain left in the hallway when the door shut behind her as she went to work. Brown eyes.

You think of your friend Delphine (who was never your friend, who was always more than your friend, since that very first day, in the café, in Montmartre, and you both knew it, though neither of you said anything then, neither of you said anything for a while yet) and you cannot remember the shape of her face, you cannot remember her jawline, or the set of her head. You remember only these fragments. A small mole on her left hip, that you would kiss. The silver ring, with black onyx set in the middle, that she took off her finger, one of those mornings, when you were lying in the bed with the white sheets, and the sun was whispering through the windows to your bare shoulder and the herringbone floor. She took the ring off her finger, and put it on the smallest finger of your left hand, and you have worn it there ever since. It is there now. You are turning the ring while you are thinking about this.

You think of your friend Delphine (who you have not seen for 51 years, since you returned to London, since you returned to Bill and to David and to this house in Notting Hill) and you know that somewhere in the house is a brown envelope filled with letters. You think there is a photo that you could look at, to remember her jaw, and the set of her head. There is an envelope somewhere in a chest of drawers, or a bureau, or a writing desk. There is an envelope that you need to find, but you cannot find. You turn the silver ring on your smallest finger, and look out of the window at the willow tree. You know that you are forgetting your friend Delphine, and you are scared.

You look around your kitchen, which is the least cluttered room in the house. In the corner, a Welsh dresser is stacked with a 12-piece dinnerware set, though you use the top two plates only. There is a dishwasher, which you never run. The drying rack next to the sink holds a mug, a side plate, a knife and fork.

The hob is old. When your son, David, comes round, you notice him watching you as you boil the kettle on the hob. Waiting to see if you will scald yourself, if you will forget to turn off the gas. He watches your hands, and you will them not to tremor as you pour the water into mugs, will them not to betray you. David has told you your kitchen is unsafe.

25

David has told you your flat is unsafe, filled with furniture that you don't use. Your bedroom used to be the dining room, and the huge walnut table is still pressed against one wall, the two side leaves permanently collapsed. Your dressing table pushed in front of it. A large armoire hulks against another wall, the top drawers open. You were looking for something in them, that you could not find. Something important. Your bed reaches out into the middle of the room. You go to sleep each night in the exact spot the table used to stand, lying out where you would once carve the roast chicken.

It is the same bed you shared with Bill, for all those years, upstairs. All those years, except for seven months. You remember the night you came back from Paris. You hadn't sent a letter, hadn't phoned ahead. You came back into the house, your key still opening the lock, and walked upstairs to where Bill, bleary with sleep, was sitting up in bed. You stood at the door, looked at him. Unsure of what was next.

"It's you," he had said. "You're back, then?" And you had nodded. That was all it was, you never spoke again about the missing months. Later in the night you had climbed the stairs to the attic room with the small child's bed and the blue gingham sheets. You remember how the moon leaked through the sash window onto your bare feet. The boy in the bed had grown in those seven months, and you were afraid to reach out and touch his hair. He turned away from you in his sleep, pulled the covers tighter. There was a sheen of night-time sweat on the nape of his neck.

As you think of this, you are fiddling with a ring on the little finger of your left hand. Twirling it round, taking it off and putting it back on again. It is silver, with black onyx set in the middle. It is a beautiful ring, and you know that it's special to you. Someone special gave it to you. You are sure.

You feel hungry, so you get up and take an apple from the fruit bowl. You peel the skin from it with an ivory-handled paring knife, that is already on the table. It reminds you of Switzerland. You peel the skin off, place it on the table in front of you. Add it to the pile of shavings that is already there. You cut the apple into slices, pressing the knife right up to your thumb.

You are looking out of the window when your son – his name is David remember? – walks into the kitchen from the hallway. He is holding a brown envelope.

"David!" you say to him. His name is David, you have remembered.

"David, where did you come from?"

He looks annoyed with you, though you don't know why. He doesn't answer, looks at you in silence, looks down to the apple peelings on the table in front of you, brown and curling.

You start to wipe them up, brushing them off the table and into your hands. You stand, walk to the food bin on the window sill, put them inside.

Your son, David, is still looking at you. You stand at the food bin, unsure what to do. Unsure why he is frowning. You stand at the food bin, looking back at him and you wait.

He tells you that he came round half an hour ago. He tells you that you answered the door to him. Told him to come in. He tells you that he is here to write a full list of the furniture, for the auction house. (He doesn't use the word "list," he says "itemise." He says he will itemise the furniture, your furniture, but you don't like that word, so you choose not to hear it.)

He tells you that you remember. He has only been out of the kitchen for 20 minutes. Of course you remember, you agree. Of course you remember.

But he is still angry, even though you have agreed. David becomes silent when he is angry, you remember that without trouble. He says nothing to you, but looks at you. So you put the lid on the food bin, put the paring knife into the sink, fill the sink with warm water and Fairy Liquid, start to wash up. You are looking out of the window. The willow tree catches your eye, as it always does. Its branches sway downwards over the pavement, kissing the heads of anyone who walks past.

Behind you, someone slams something onto your formica table. You look around, and your son, David, is there. He has put a brown paper envelope on the table and he looks furious.

You recognise the envelope. It looks old. You know the handwriting on the front; it makes you feel happy to see it, though the reason why is just out of reach. It has been written in blue ink, but is very faded. Your name is on the front. Leonora. Your name and your address, here in Notting Hill.

You reach out for the envelope, which is thick, stuffed full, which must have many things inside. There is a tear down the side seam at one edge. It is addressed to you and you want to open it.

You pick up the envelope, your pink octagonal bangle knocking against your wrist. As you pull the flap open, there is a very faint smell of Guerlain. You are smiling, when David punches the table with his fist.

You look up at him.

He has both hands on your formica table, is leaning over it towards you. He tells you to concentrate.

You are holding a brown envelope, full of paper, with one seam split. You look at the envelope and see that it is shaking, that your hands are shaking. You will your hands not to betray you.

But David, who is leaning across the table, is shaking too. His neck is red. He wants you to explain to him just what is the meaning of these letters in this envelope.

But you cannot.
You cannot.

In Time

by Francis McCrickard

Second Prize, Edinburgh Flash Fiction Award 2024

She was me mother but that was the first time I'd *studied* her.

Deft, I suppose, is the word. *Over, under*; steady, sure. She did a lot of it, the sewing. Turning shirt collars, patching jeans, making Christmas stockings for us, little dresses and, one time, a quilt from all kinds of material. And socks: darning. Same thing, I suppose. All by hand, needles bristling on *Ma's hedgehog*, the wee cushion she made from scraps and stuffing. She even embroidered an altar cloth for down the road. We went into Outer Space under it as she sewed big red letters on the white strip: *SANCTUS SANCTUS SANCTUS.*

'Genius with them fingers,' somebody said at a family do.

'A lovely touch those fingers have,' Da added. He winked at her. She frowned and then smiled.

Long, thin fingers my mother has but like padlocks on wrists I remember when we walked past the checkpoints to the shops or school.

She can do all them fancy stitches: *cross, chain, blanket. Blind*'s another. This wasn't *blind*. Over, under; over, under.

She used a local linen thread she told me was fine but strong and really for shoes or maybe chairs.

I didn't think she'd let me watch.

'Old enough,' Da said.

'A sad reality,' she said. *Over, under.*

McCann fainted a couple of times, shuddered and came round again. Ma tied a knot deftly, cut the thread, breathed deeply.

Da gave me the stubby bullet, deformed, he said, by striking the bone.

See The Light Play on the Water

by Rob Schofield

Third Prize, Edinburgh Short Story Award 2024

Black mould and fungi are killing kids. I used to wonder about the mushrooms under the window, but it turns out they're real. I shut them into the flat, press my back to the door and breathe, but the smell's no better in the hall. There are two dead plants at the bottom of the staircase, dribbling soil onto the carpet. Outside 1A is a bike that's missing a wheel, and there's a scooter that someone's messed with by the fire escape. They've all got them and fuck all's being done about it.

The street is dark. Clouds have got the better of the sun, but it's lurking, waiting for an opportunity. It's good to know it's risen. The promise of warmth and light keeps me moving. I know where I'm going, but I've somewhere to be first. I choose to hope the sky will be blue by the time I reach my destination.

Number 8's bin is on its side next to a mound of dogshit that reminds me of clay on a potter's wheel. The bin's empty, so I pick it up and trundle it back from where it came. That's what Mum would have done. Some of the shite has got on the wheels, and it leaves a trail for the owners, should they be interested in its journey. Being curious is a way of staying in the moment. You can take that too far, like how a bin got to where it was and back again, how it got shit on its wheels, and what sort of person lets their mutt evacuate in the centre of a busy path. Okay, it was sloppy, but it was a choice not to clean it up.

Six people are queuing for the bus. Two look asleep, two are twitching, trying to see around a corner, and the other two are locked on their phones. The fact that they're in pairs makes the back of my neck tingle. Seven's a lucky number, but I won't be the odd one at the bus stop. I keep walking and that's when I bump into Chrissy.

She's begging next to the Spar. She's so spaced out she doesn't realise the cash machine's out of order. You can't deny she's got a killer smile. If she'd been born someone else, she'd have perfect skin and would be a model. She'd still be skinny, which is ironic and tragic. Two for one, like the Strongbow in the Spar. Howdy, she says, in a cowboy voice. She mustn't know it's me. She doesn't like to waste her charms. Chrissy, I say, it's me. She puts a hand to her eyes like a salute. Nails black and bitten. Thumb bleeding. She smiles, and I see the gaps where a model would never have teeth missing. Spare some change, pardner, she says. Chrissy, I say, it's me. She lowers her hand and drops her chin to her chest. I leave my bus fare between her feet.

Auntie Karen is in her coat, slippers and pjs underneath. Mum told me to look out for her. She used to be fierce, Mum once said, but now's she's fragile. Show me someone who isn't, is how I wish I could reply. Auntie Karen wants to know about the weather. If she pulled the curtains back, she could see for herself. I describe it better than it looks, she says. She gives me a twenty for the messages. Bacon, spuds, a piece of fish and some peas. Milk. Tea bags. The cheap ones. Five pounds on the leccy. A quarter bottle if there's enough. She sends me next door for a mug of hot water. She can't get going without her morning brew.

I won't go back to the Spar because a) Chrissy, and b) I'm trying to move forwards today. It's quiet in Lidl, but it takes me ages because I don't know where stuff is. There's a long queue when I get to the till. How can that be? I've seen two people with baskets and that's it. I'm next but one in line when the cashier goes on a break. The new one looks familiar. I might have been at school with him. He doesn't let on. It comes to me when I'm outside: not his name, but who he is. No wonder he kept schtum. A conspiracy of silence, ten or fifteen years later. Who am I kidding? Eleven years and three months. Someone should have spoken up, but we were kids. Teenagers is still kids.

Hang on. He's followed me out. He tugs my elbow from behind. Whoa, I say. Don't touch me. Sorry, he says, I'm the same. I was always like that, I says, but I know what you mean. He's still around, he says. Our kid's seen him. His kid was good at footy, and with girls. Nobody messed with him. Where, I says. My balls tighten and I can't get my breath. In town, he says. With a crowd of hangers on. No change there then, I say. Looks like shite now. Drinker's nose apparently. That's good, I says, pinching my snout. Never touch the stuff. After your Mum, he asks, and then clamps a mitt around his gob. Sorry. Don't worry, I says. People never know what to say. Something's better than nothing.

His hands are on his hips. You'd think he'd have learned it's not a good look. He's watching me as I turn onto a street where the houses are neat and tidy, with front gardens. Real and artificial grass. Decking. Fountains and ponds. A gang of sparrows in a hedge. If there's a pecking order, I can't work it out. They're noisy buggers. With all that energy, if they got organised, they could achieve something. As it is, they'll get no further than food, water, and shelter in the hedge or thereabouts. A hand flashes through a blind. I point at the birds. The hand retreats and I take my cue.

Cars parked on the pavement, facing forward. Princess on board. Football teams. Flags. A smiley face. A finger or two.

Danny Swift, that was him, at Lidl. Funny how your name doesn't always fit. Swift he was not. Two scooters pass in a blur. I grip the shopping bag. I didn't see their faces, but I bet their hoods were pulled into tight circles. Threats of moustaches on top of skinny lips. Terrified, wannabe gangsters. Children. Could have been me. Or you. A dog barks, and then another. A cat dozes in a window. The sparrows are safe for now.

Auntie Karen's tied an apron over her coat. Sit down, she says, I'm making breakfast. I've eaten, I lie. Well you can eat again, she says, no arguments. Bacon butties. Put a bag in the teapot. Rinse that mug under the tap. I take a moment to feel my seat, wiggle my toes, squeeze and relax my fists. Breathe in for five and out for eight. I'd do eleven, but I don't want to freak her out. I open my eyes and a shaft of sun has got through her nets. This makes me uneasy because I want to get where I'm going. I don't want to miss my chance. This is what today is supposed to be about. Auntie Karen puts two plates on the table. I toasted the bread, she says. No brown sauce. Fine by me, I says, I'm red all the way. Your mum was red too, she says, and winks. She's wrong, but I don't want to burst her bubble. It's better to be nice than right.

Auntie Karen dabs the crumbs from her plate and lights up. She blows a long plume to the ceiling. Ahh, she says. Two a day now. One after breakfast and one after tea. What about lunch? She inhales and shakes her head. I don't to want to come between her and her ciggy, so I stare through the nets. The clouds are in retreat. The sun is asserting itself. All it had to do, like the rest of us, was wait. Earth calling. Earth calling, she says as she extinguishes the cigarette. I can hear the crush under her thumb. Tobacco smudging plate, deprived of oxygen. The last throes of a killer. What are you frowning for? I'm not. You are. Am I? Yes. Just thinking. You're always thinking. I'm a thinker, what can I say? You're a dreamer is what you are. No, I say. Dreams are for other people. Here and now, that's what I'm about. You don't ever think of your mum? I scrape the plates into the bin and leave them by the sink. Places to go, people to see, Auntie K. She opens her arms for a hug. Who do you have to see, she whispers into my ear. I kiss her cheek. Well, there's you.

Downhill from here, but I'm upbeat. Excited. If an alien landed now, they wouldn't have to find a word for clouds. They'd have a quick mooch and fuck back off. It takes a lifetime to appreciate this world of ours. If you get that long. If you work on it, the warmth of the sun can mask a thousand cruelties. Don't waste time on potter's wheels filled with dogshit. Forget about gangs on e-bikes. Put Daniel not-so-Swift out of your mind. Stay grounded. Breathe from your diaphragm. Think of people and things that matter. Chrissy. Auntie Karen. Mum.

From where I'm standing, I can see it through a gap between the warehouses at the bottom of the hill. It disappears as I descend. Don't rush, don't dawdle. Imagine what is to come. Paint a positive picture in your mind and half the battle's won, ere the set of sun. Flashbacks to school. That's Swifty's fault, coming out of the past in Lidl. One warehouse is 'To Let'. The other's a radiator outlet, vintage and new. There's some of us scared of putting the heating on while others are reclaiming ironwork from office blocks and old churches. Slap cheeks twice.

There's a busy road to cross. Drivers not inclined to slow. I can see it now, on the other side and behind a fence. A solid grey/blue mass, like a swollen oblong trying to escape its shackles. There's a way down to the path, but I can't figure out where it is. Traffic lights must have changed somewhere, and I make it over the road. Fuck it: I climb the fence, swaying with the wire. It's a wrestling match and I win. A patch of land, which could be a skate park or basketball court. They could build a library. A health centre. As it is, it's a place for litter to gather. Cans, packets, bags. A withered hose. At the end, a low wall to clamber over that's been tagged, and tagged over the tag.

Mum taught me to look for the beauty in life. This is where I find it. She liked poetry, and I feel her whenever I come down to the river. I love how the breeze riffles the water into millions of gleaming jewels. When the sun disappears, I'm reminded that things don't last, even if they sometimes come back. Once, it was so cold that sheets of ice jostled the banks. When the wind blows hard from the city, I imagine it's carrying away the stuff we don't want or need: violence, fear, ignorance, hate, hunger, despair, black mould and fungi. I think about all of it breaking down amongst the vastness of the ocean; and when it blows the other way, what will it bring us? Mum, come hold my hand. I'd give everything I'll ever own for you to see the light play on the water.

The Good Storyteller

by Terri Mullholland

Third Prize, Edinburgh Flash Fiction Award 2024

You're telling me a story like the good storyteller you are. But you're playing hide and seek in the spaces between words. In the gap between where the story starts and where it ends you're dancing around, drawing things out.

I'm impatient. I want you to get straight to the heart of the tale, the meat of it, the bit where things happen.

But you're taking your time, carefully setting things up, laying the table for the Once Upon A Time. You're straightening the tablecloth, arranging the plates, the glassware – getting everything ready to bring in the Happily Ever After on a platter.

You've even put a vase of wildflowers on the table, picked just for me in the woods this morning. But I'm still waiting for you to get past what happened after you entered the woods and followed the path to the cottage. What happened after the wolf opened the door?

I know you must have escaped because here you are, telling me the story as you polish the silver cutlery.

But now you're setting out a knife and fork at a place setting for one, and you're looking at me with those hungry eyes, and I realise you're not going to tell me what happened next. Like the good storyteller you are, you're going to show me.

Wing Mirrors

by Frances McKendrick

Winner, Isobel Lodge Award for Unpublished Writers in Scotland

We're inside a roofless cage in some shithole suburb made beautiful by this unusually glorious summer. Dead centre of a cloudless blue sky, the sun's beating down on tatty turf-burn astro; parents, sweltering in the wrong gear, too hot to chat, lean uncomfortably or shadow restless toddlers along the sidelines.

Sid's waiting in position for the starting whistle, coltish on his skinny eight-year-old legs, eager to run, to kick, to trap; the back of his slender neck the origin of a jolt of searing tenderness felt in my throat. I swallow hard, shove it down. I'm glad we're here. I mean, why should he have missed out today? Again.

She shouldn't even *be* at home.

Little bitch.

Beneath my t-shirt the prickle-soak of sweat already gone sour. I should've showered; my hygiene another victim of her disgusting disease.

I'd walked out the door, away from the sight of her.

The state of her.

Sunday morning people, dogs, and joggers, hair-of-the-doggers; as we sat at traffic lights the harsh angles of her stubborn wraith-face replicated in everyone who passed.

I'd swiped at my tears with windscreen-wiper hands. Jabbed at the stereo.

Let's put the radio on, eh, sweetie? Get some tunes going, eh Sid?

Sid's half smile in the rearview mirror. His *okay mum* had no heart in it. It was only then that I'd noticed his hair, whipped into stiff meringue-like peaks, glistening with wax; presumably a homage to some footballer of whose style I'm unaware.

Love your hair baby!

He'd winced. What had seemed a good idea, a little experimenting with some hair product first thing on a hopeful match-day morning, after the upsetting scene in the house, now a toe-curling vainglorious mistake.

Why should *he* have to live a life suspended?

Little no-bother Sid.

In comparison.

She is bother, but then she was our first.

Why won't Coach blow the starting whistle?

It's so hot. I smell like salt and vinegar crisps.

And they're off.

Sid breaks up the left wing, circumnavigates an equally gangly opposition midfielder with fox-coloured hair, only to have his feet taken out from under him by a prune-faced defender in a too tight strip. Sausage boy won't last the first half in this heat.

Nice. Slagging off someone else's child; and for their weight no less.

Glass houses.

I had not realised just how fragile our house was. How little a splinter was needed to cause the whole thing to shatter.

WING MIRRORS! shouts Coach

Coach doesn't shut up, but it's what they need. His instructions keeping the ball at their feet, threading their passes between them; without his voice they'd unravel.

Not to mention that sculpted body...

We – me, Sid, and Coach – could make a new home, solid, built of bricks, no amount of huffing and puffing would shift it.

Jesus, it's actually baking hot. I never thought to put cream on Sid.

A new life with lovely Coach. No ghouls, no soup poured down the sides of shoes, yoghurt hidden in straw hair. Just everyone strong and vital, and steak and chips and holidays and Nat 5's and friends and parties and....

Her face inside my eyelids and her name a stain a bruise a curse in my mouth.

She isn't even supposed to be at home.

She didn't have to do that this morning. Didn't have to sabotage our Sunday.

What do you do with a baby? my husband, Sandy, had asked when I got pregnant the first time.

I'd laughed, said, you just love it, I think.

WING MIRRORS!

If I was married to Coach, I'd ban him from shouting that.

And we'd loved her. Oh, how we loved her.

I never saw it coming.

How could I not have seen it coming?

As a younger child she was sylphic under a cloud of blonde hair. People would comment on her beauty, and I'd feel sorry for the mums with the plain bairns. Then thirteen hit, and she got hips and tits and verdigris-green streaks through a choppy bob and all over the shower-tile grouting. I could've killed her. Prostrate on the kitchen lino, wailing about having body odour, body hair, and period pain and, really, just how *minging* it was, *all this bloody bleeding!* She'd arrived in puberty like a mid-explosion bomb, and she was hilariously funny. Her room smelt like old bin, and she did terrible things like scooshing deodorant on her legs and igniting it with a lighter just to shock Sid, who loved to be shocked.

Sandy could've killed her.

At the dinner table she talked incessantly. Whip-smart vignettes about her teachers, fellow students, and my concentration wandered because post-work I was knackered, but when it returned, Sid and Sandy would be laughing, great fat belly-laughs, and she'd be pink with the pleasure of her own burgeoning, blossoming mind. Drunk on her own juices.

WING MIRRORS!

If he yells that one more time...

I swig from Sid's bottle as the half-time whistle blows.

Are they getting beat?

Sid's lowered chin says it all. Scuffing up plastic soil as he shoulder-rolls over for his bottle. My boy needs a win.

Doing great baby!

Hot as a boiled egg he sluices water down his neck before dashing back to Coach for their half-time pep talk.

I blamed Sandy first.

Then the school.

The internet.

Society.

Andrew Tate.

Eventually she told us of a boy in her year she'd liked, whose fingers she'd felt encircling her upper arm in the melee of the school corridor. He with his mates, laughing, jostling, streaming past her, she with her headphones on, in her own world, and suddenly the warmth of his touch, unexpected and dreamlike – dreamt-of. Then they were ahead of her, and she'd removed a headphone, smiled his way and he'd smiled back, held up his hand in the imprint of her bicep, a gap before his fingers met, disconnecting the circle, which he pointed to with the other hand and called, *hey Miss Piggy, maybe time to lay off the doughnuts...*

That was the chink, the tear, all that was needed.

My anger scorched everyone and everything it touched, until it burned itself out and left me with something far worse.

Has Sid drunk enough water? He has a habit of spitting out as the pros do. Daft boy.

Some girls just get lost in it, the duty psychiatrist said, as if my daughter had simply been wandering through a forest.

She didn't get lost in her illness – it invaded her, snapping and snarling. Found the breach, moved in, and took over, perverted and warped her, messed with all her settings until she moved to a new beat, rotated on a new axis. Barely recognisable, unknowable; there but not there. Alive but not living.

How could my girl, our girl...

Humans are heat engines, if you don't put in enough fuel, the fire goes out.

The whistle blows. Second half is on.

First, they reduced her timetable. Soon after, it was decided she could no longer go to school. We fought and fought for help that never came, because of, you know – waiting lists.

I took to listening at the frosted windowpane in the bathroom door, then in a moment of madness removed the entire thing from its hinges, till Sandy, ever the human rights defender, pointed out that my actions were against hers. And anyway, she'd just puke in the bin, or one of the many plastic bags she had secreted around the house.

Whittling away at herself from the inside, so obviously blighted on the outside, eventually she was sectioned under the mental health act, spirited away to a psychiatric unit, and forcibly fed through a tube that they'd pushed up her nose and into her stomach against her will. Which, for her, was akin to being violently assaulted by the same people who were watching her use the toilet, eat, shower, and sleep.

And we, her doting parents, let them. We were relieved.

Family therapy, psychotherapy, dialectical behaviour therapy: promising, muscular sounding interventions which never even touched the sides.

Before, she'd been as bright, and often as unwatchable, as a magnesium flare. The first, always, to take up any kind of challenge. One summer, in agony after dislocating her shoulder during a harbour jump, en route to the Infirmary she belted out a full-throated *Oh Flower of Scotland* just so that Sid wouldn't realise the extent of her suffering and get upset. During a holiday up north, she emerged blithe and beatific from a tangle of thorny dogrose so fierce that she resembled the recipient of an over-zealous stigmata. 'Nutter!' Sandy had shouted proudly. Only a black magic of unutterable cruelty could change a girl like *that* to this extent.

They discharged her the first and every other time, not because she had improved, but because 'we require the bed' for some other creature *worse than her*. There are no specialist eating disorder units left in Scotland, and so the adolescent psych unit at the local hospital is my baby's second home now.

WING MIRRORS!

Focus!

My boy sends a perfect pass to the striker who volleys it into the far corner of the net – top bins! Sid, jubilant, leaps into the air. Whole and perfect.

I will not think of her alone in our house. Sandy's shift will be over soon, and he'll go straight home.

I will stay mad. I will cruise on this bad energy.

Sid turns and beams and I thrust out my upturned thumb, *Yes Sid!*

CENTRE CIRCLE! bellows Coach.

It's so damn hot.

This morning, after the screaming, she'd whimpered it: *why don't you care about me anymore?* and I'd closed the door on her skin and bones, on her strange over-ripe peaches smell, because by then I'd harnessed enough rage, enough righteousness to get me and Sid out into the sunshine and away from the spectre that is left of her.

She'll be back in the unit soon enough.

The psychologist suggested Sid was in danger of becoming a *Glass Child.*

WING MIRRORS!

What does that even mean? Something to do with the wingers?

A *Glass Child* is the emotionally neglected sibling of a child with a disability or illness, who people tend to see right through. Appearing resilient, happy and problem-free, really they are as breakable as an antique bauble fallen from a Christmas tree.

As if I didn't feel guilty enough. I cringed at every time I'd cheerfully told folk how little bother my son was, clinging, limpet-like, to what I thought were the positives.

Some girls just get lost in it.

Glass child.

These are my children you are talking about, my babies.

We're only trying to help.

Sandy had let me take it out on him. Then he'd said gently: *The guys a prick, Sid's no glass child. I get that it's a thing, but Sid doesn't fit the profile, and we'll make sure he never does.*

Sandy has a way of taking my fears and repurposing them, handing them back to me with the bite taken out.

I'm not sure Coach could do that.

The whistle blows. Thank God.

Sid bounds over victorious and sweaty, and I'm spent with the effort of staying angry. The rage has evaporated and now the ache for her is blooming outward, as it always does.

Sid, what does Coach mean when he shouts wing mirrors?

Aw mum, it's obvious – he means look around you! Scan the pitch, read the game. Keep your head up!

Of course.

Keep your head up.

What do you think Sid? Celebratory ice cream at Valdini's? Shall we sit in for once?

Do you want to stretch this moment out, pretend a little longer?

Nah mum, take-away. I know she probably won't eat it, but I think we should get her some Raspberry Ripple just in case, because it's her favourite, and you never know...

His clear-eyed, hopeful, beautiful face. All heart.

I smile.

You're right my love, you never know...

The Outlier

by Allison Brisbane

Winner, Golden Hare Award for Scottish Flash Fiction, 2024

'You're sure this time?'

'Reasonably sure, Captain.'

'Listen up, Lieutenant Schnurgh, once I secrete our home coordinates there's no returning to this utter butt-gusset of a planet for 117.2 light years. So, are you *entirely* sure you've *definitively* obtained a superior specimen of the highest life-form?'

'Yes, Captain.'

'Surer than when you obtained the previous specimens?' the captain sneered, eye-stalks swivelling towards a budgie, a coelacanth, and a Henry the Hoover.

'Y...yes,' stuttered Schnurgh, plasma glands leaching tendrils of mucus into orbit around his vestigial proboscis.

The captain raised a sceptical mandible. 'Because...?'

'...having found the highest life-form, after anal probing of multiple samples to confirm the presence of brain-matter, I tested at global population level for superior processing ability.'

'By...?'

'...developing an algorithm to elicit the interest and participation of the most intelligent specimens.'

'Then...?'

'...ranking subjects who performed best to identify one whose cerebral acumen exceeded all others.'

'And...?'

'...beaming it aboard.'

'Finally,' muttered the captain, his carunculated sphincter puckering moistly above the navigation controls.

Glasgow Evening Times: 'Concern Grows for Missing Woman'
The distressed daughter of Mrs Thomasina McTurk (83) from Whifflet, told our reporter, 'I rang Mum the night before but when I went round the next day, her glasses and the *People's Friend* were lying on the bedspread and she'd – disappeared. Hadn't taken her teeth or slippers or anything. I'll never forget the last thing she said, 'Jeannie, guess what? That's me, got the Wordle in two, again.'

Takeout Chinese Near Me

by Franky Seymour

Winner, Write Mango Short Story Award 2024

Friday, June 7th, 2024

17:34	what to wear on a first date
17:35	what to wear on a first date, guy
17:37	what to wear on a first date, no time to buy new clothes
17:42	untucked shirt over 30, ok?
17:44	does doing your top button up make you a hipster
17:45	what colour shirt says "interesting young professional"
17:45	is interesting young professional an oxymoron
17:46	define oxymoron
17:46	define moron
20:01	what wine is good wine
20:02	what wine is good wine, under $20
20:08	is any wine good wine under $20
20:08	how to drink bad wine and not let it show
20:41	how to tell if a date is going well
20:42	define connection
20:43	define spark
20:45	define awkward silence
21:03	good topics of conversation for dates
21:14	is more than 3 trips to the bathroom a bad sign?
21:19	can one bring up a bladder infection over dinner?
21:38	what is astrology, brief explanation

21:41	is it rude to correct a date's misunderstanding of basic scientific principles?
21:43	how long does it take for awkward silence to become weird
22:43	takeout chinese for one, near me

Saturday, June 8th, 2024

18:34	dating apps for guys over 30
18:46	dating apps for guys over 30, not just looking for sex
19:02	what does netflix and chill actually mean?
20:23	is getting a cat weird for a single guy
23:08	takeout chinese for one, near me

Monday, June 10th, 2024

09:53	dating sites for successful businessmen
09:54	dating sites for businessmen
09:55	dating sites for men who work in business
09:55	does working as a bank teller count as working in business
10:11	how to write a good dating profile
10:15	s it ok to lie about your hobbies on match.com
10:16	what hobbies make a person sound interesting
10:25	how soon is too soon to admit I like dungeons and dragons?
21:43	takeout chinese for one, near me

Wednesday, June 12th, 2024

16:26	first dates, how to learn from your mistakes
16:28	first dates, he picked the venue, is that ok?

16:33	first date at a bar, should I bring flowers
16:34	first date at a bar, should I bring friends?
16:52	how early is too early to turn up to a date?
20:51	he laughs at my jokes, good or bad sign?
20:53	what does it mean if he smiles when I talk
20:55	how to not get distracted by someone's eyes when they're speaking
20:58	is it possible for a person to be too beautiful?
20:59	how to stop yourself from saying what you're thinking out loud
22:28	is letting your date punch someone a bad idea?
22:29	how to avoid starting fights in LA dive bars
22:33	does getting thrown out of a bar give you a criminal record?
23:12	can you catch dengue fever from a public fountain
23:13	how can someone look more beautiful soaking wet
23:28	how soon is too soon to tell him you love him
23:29	are engagement rings misogynistic?
23:32	what does it mean that I would do anything he asked?
|	
23:29	takeout chinese for two, near me

Thursday, June 13th, 2024

09:52	second date, help!
09:53	second date, what does it mean?
10:04	second date at lunch, romantic ideas
10:06	second date at lunch, does this make him my boyfriend?
10:34	is it ok to propose while eating deli sandwiches

13:36	he wants to see where I work, good sign?
13:36	he wants to see where I work, bad sign?
13:43	can making out at work get you fired
13:45	is it ok to propose in a supply closet
13:46	is it ok to propose while showing him the vaults
14:14	silent alarm, deactivate?
14:14	silent alarm, off, how?
14:15	is it still a silent alarm if it's making a lot of noise
14:20	how to control a large group of people
14:21	how to keep control of a large group of people
14:22	do they still count as hostages if you know all their names
14:26	how to make it look like you have a gun in your pocket
14:27	what does it mean if your boyfriend has a gun in his pocket
14:31	fisherman's knots, simple tutorial
14:32	tying up your coworkers quickly
14:33	bondage for beginners, but not the kinky stuff
14:39	how heavy is gold IRL
14:39	should a man over 30 say IRL
14:39	how to tell your boyfriend he looks beautiful in strobe lighting
14:41	safe deposit boxes, quick guide
14:42	safe deposit boxes, i've lost my key
14:43	safe deposit boxes, not very secure
14:44	safe deposit boxes, do they all contain diamonds?
14:46	money laundering, the basics

16:57	Bonnie and Clyde, happy ending?
17:11	he says we should meet in mexico, should I make reservations?
17:12	romantic getaway for two, cancellation policy preferred
17:13	LA to mexico by helicopter
17:13	LA to mexico on foot
17:13	LA to mexico, uber?
17:14	do they have takeout chinese in cancun?
17:47	best law firm in LA
17:49	adequate law firms in LA
17:52	are court-appointed lawyers really that bad
17:53	does the "distract and slip away" plan ever work out well for the distraction
18:26	when they say "come out with your hands up", do they mean it literally?
18:27	what does it say about me that I still don't regret this?

Friday, June 14th, 2024

19:31	takeout chinese for one, near California State Correctional, delivery preferred

For All Rats to Read

by Nicola Caroli

Winner, Write Mango Flash Award 2024

As souls of dead rats may warn the living of danger or death, one should warn rats – preferably by written notice – that you will destroy them if they return.

For All Rats to Read

I have a big tomcat called Tom. He wears blue crinkled leather boots over his paws and an awesome vermillion scarf flung around his neck. At nineteen years old, he's at the height of his prowling prowess. Rats are a pleasant distraction for him; they remind him of the small mice he had for breakfast when he was young. When he gets a whiff of a rat under the floorboards or hears a heavy scurry in the attic, he puts on the small onyx cross his mother gave him before she died and disappears for an extremely short time. On his return, which is victorious on principle rather than by decree, I serve salmon carpaccio. I stock it in the freezer in large quantities. He looks at me across the table as if I were one of the grey, ugly, fat-arsed creatures he just tore apart without getting his boots dirty or disturbing the verve of his scarf. During dinner I say his name one hundred times. Then I smoke a joint and listen to the Sex Pistols, gazing at the swaying white curtain in front of the tall open window. I imagine Tom tells me he loves me, and I tell him I love him too.

Penguins and Empanadas

by Catherine Varley

Highly Commended, Edinburgh Short Story Award 2024

Mary looked longingly at the empanadas on the adjacent table. The crisp, golden pastry and delicately crimped edges, each one promising a different combination of the strong Argentinian flavours that so delighted her taste buds. Across from her, Roger studied the menu with such intent that, for a moment, she could almost imagine that he was interested in the food. Then he got out his calculator.

'Some of the main courses are quite good value, but the side dishes are an absolute rip off,' he said, without looking up.

'I thought we could try the empanadas to start?'
'Empanadas?'

'Yes, they're little pastry...' her voice trailed off into nothing as Roger interrupted.

'I am well aware, Mary, of what an empanada is.' He made no effort to pronounce the word in Spanish, he never did, as if by doing so would be a step too far in culinary exploration. 'I do not see why we should pay £4.50 for a handful of undersized Cornish pasties. And you know my views on starters.'

Mary knew very well Roger's views on starters, to the extent that he had once had her type up a letter to the Surrey Advertiser on the subject. Roger believed that starters were a conspiracy of the restaurant industry, allowing them to increase profits by reducing main portion sizes and forcing customers to buy two courses. It was a matter of great pride for Roger that he had never in his life paid for a starter.

The arrival of the waiter rescued her from his usual diatribe, and she sat back as Roger ordered them both the cheapest thing on the menu and a bottle of still water. She recalled how, on the first night, he had tried to persuade the waiter to bring them a jug of tap water. It was only the threat of E-coli that had persuaded him to pay for water in restaurants since. In the hotel, however, she was forced to boil the kettle.

'I'm looking forward to tomorrow,' Mary said, straightening her knife and fork in anticipation of her omelette. 'What time do we leave?'

'It says 9am on the itinerary, but I'd like us to be ready by 8.30. Breakfast at 7.30.'

Since they'd arrived in Argentina, the all-inclusive breakfast had become Mary's favourite meal of the day. Today, however, as she loaded her tray with bacon and eggs, fruit and pastries, her focus turned to the group excursion. It was Roger's only reason for having made the costly trip in the first place, the chance to see some condors in their natural habitat. Mary was more excited about the penguins.

Roger was already halfway through his breakfast, his hand in the air to summon the waitress for more coffee, his mouth too full to manage more than a grunt of acknowledgement when it arrived. He pointed at the empty bowl which had, on previous mornings, contained a number of small bread rolls. The waitress understood the gesture and took it to be replenished.

'Were there none?' Mary asked, reaching for the pepper. Roger didn't like pepper. It was too spicy for him.

'There were, but they're in the bag,' Roger said, with a surreptitious nod towards his daypack.

'They're what?'

'They're in the bag,' he whispered, 'for later. Now, I need you to go and help yourself to some of the continental, you know, the cheese and meats.'

'But I don't want cheese and meats,' Mary replied, 'I've got bacon and eggs.'

'It's not for now, it's for later – I'm going to make us sandwiches.'

This was a new low for Roger and, in Mary's opinion, tantamount to theft, but she did as she was told and returned to the counter, loading her plate with sweaty cheese slices and processed ham. Her fellow holidaymakers watched as she headed back to the table, her precarious mountain of sandwich fillers leading the way. She could hear them whispering, something about an eating disorder, 'a little bird of a thing like that'. She had hoped that this trip might be different, that she might have made some friends, but Roger's antics had put a stop to any chance of that.

The first night, they had been on a table with the rest of the group, Mary sandwiched between a jolly gay man with a beard, who worked in television, and delightful widow who had recently moved to Oxford. Roger had been safely ensconced at the other end of the table, and Mary had enjoyed herself immensely until pudding, at which point he had come to join her – likely, she had thought at the time, to ensure she hadn't ordered any. On discovering the widow's recent loss, Roger had expressed his sympathy and, for a brief moment, Mary had let herself relax. It soon transpired, however, that Roger's sympathy related only to the fact that the widow would be forever more at the mercy of the dreaded Single Person Supplement. There were times that Mary wondered whether, just perhaps, the Single Person Supplement was the only reason Roger had married her in the first place.

The conversation became no less strained when the bill arrived, which everyone else had been happy to split. Roger's refusal to do so (they, of course, had only had mains), and the ensuing row, had ruined any chance Mary had of making friends within the group. As she watched him now, shovelling muesli into his mouth, her focus drawn to the small piece of dried fruit which had adhered itself to the corner of his lip, she wondered how much longer she could stand it.

The view from the cliffs had been astonishing, and well worth the effort. Roger had been so absorbed by the birds that Mary had been able to spend time on her own, exploring the rocky outcrops and looking down towards the crashing waves, and the tiny black and white dots of penguins leaping in and out of the water.

There was much talk of the day's lunch stop, which was to be an asado, the traditional Argentinian barbecue. Mary had read about them in the guidebooks, leisurely afternoons spent beside the warmth of the large open fire, feasting on beef, pork, ribs, sausages and sweetbreads hot off the grill. She had been looking forward to it for much of the week however, as she saw Roger in deep conversation with the guide, her heart fell and the significance of the home made breakfast-sandwiches dawned on her.

'Marvellous news,' said Roger, as he approached, binoculars dangling from his thick, red neck, 'they've agreed that we can have a ten percent discount on today's outing if we agree not to have the lunch.'

'But I was rather looking forward to it,' Mary said, hesitantly, 'and it was in the holiday budget.'

'Yes, I know it was originally, but I went slightly over on these binoculars, so we need to balance things out.'

'But...'

'It's okay, you can use them for a bit if you like, what's mine is yours and all that!' He gave her arm a perfunctory squeeze, before walking away, his stubby little fingers leaving an impression on her padded coat that disappeared as quickly as he did.

Mary could see the smoke from the parrilla curling up from the beach, the smell reaching over the rocks and up towards where she stood. It couldn't hurt, she thought, to go and have a look. To stand and watch the others as they piled their plates high with chorizos, mollejas and morcilla, enjoying these smaller, more delicate cuts, while they waited for the main event. She slid cautiously down the grassy embankment, towards a group of fellow travellers who had already helped themselves and were now discussing the merits of chimichurri sauce.

'It's delicious, and so easy to make,' said one.

'Too spicy for me,' said another, 'all that raw garlic too, just think about your breath!'

Mary thought about Roger's breath. He never ate anything remotely garlicky, yet still managed to have the worst breath of any man she knew. A few mouthfuls of chimichurri might actually be an improvement. Behind the chattering group, Mary could see a man in chef's whites sharpening a large knife. A small crowd was gathering and, as she stepped nearer, she could see what appeared to be a small pig on a spit adjacent to the open grill. The smell was incredible, and as the chef leaned over the hot coals to cut the first slice of pork, she heard the satisfying snap of perfect crackling and her mouth watered.

'Mary!'

She looked up to see Roger standing on the embankment, waving a carrier bag, and her heart sank. The thought of stale bread rolls and that unnaturally pink ham, if you could call it ham, did nothing to hasten her steps up the hill. The chatter of the other people on the beach behind her, the wonderful smell of roasting meat, it was all she could do not to stamp her foot and scream at the unfairness of it all.

Roger had spread his coat on the ground like a picnic rug, and as he handed her the excuse for a lunch, the smug look on his face made her want to punch him hard on the nose.

'See, who needs all that nonsense? A simple ham and cheese roll is all you need.'

Mary said nothing for a while, she simply sat there staring out to sea, watching the penguins in the water.

'Could I borrow the binoculars for a moment, Roger?'

'Of course dear, here you go, do you want me to show you how to use them?'

'No thank you, I'm perfectly capable.' Mary raised the binoculars and looked out towards the rocks. She couldn't believe she hadn't seen them before, they were huge, beastlike creatures. They reminded her slightly of Roger's sister. 'What is it?' asked Roger, unused to such self-assurance from Mary.

'Sea lions,' said Mary. Something else caught Mary's eye. 'I'm going to go and have a look,' she said, standing up and brushing herself down.

'Aren't you going to finish your sandwich?'

'I'll take it with me.'

Mary reached the rocky outcrop and looked around, but there was no sign of the man in the uniform she'd seen patrolling moments earlier. Back up the hill she could just make out Roger, still sitting on his coat, watching her through his precious, over-budget binoculars. She took a few steps towards the terrifying wildlife, but there was no reaction from them, they simply continued to lie there, writhing occasionally. One gave an impressive yawn.

'Madam! Madam, please!' The man in the uniform had appeared from wherever he'd been hiding. 'Madam, you must come away from the sea lions, they are very dangerous at this time of year!'

Mary stopped and turned towards the man, she could see from the badge on his uniform that his name was Pablo. He had the words Park Ranger emblazoned underneath.

'You must come away please, madam, you did not see the sign?'

Mary had, of course, seen the sign. She had seen the sign from the safety of Roger's makeshift picnic blanket. It was enormous.

'I'm so sorry, how stupid of me,' Mary said, as she backed slowly away from the sea lions. 'It's just, I wanted to give them this.' And with that, she threw her partially eaten ham and cheese roll into the writhing masses.

Climbing down from the rocks, towards the officious looking Park Ranger, Mary looked up to make sure Roger was still watching. She needn't have worried, even without binoculars it was apparent that he had seen it all, including the sign:

DANGEROUS ANIMALS

KEEP AWAY

DO NOT FEED

FINE $1000

Snow Wine

by Brian Sneeden

Highly Commended, Edinburgh Flash Fiction Award 2024

To sanitise the vineyard we halve a pomegranate with a paring knife and walk in circles flicking seeds. In the *Papyri Graecae Magicae* a white rooster is preferred, gripped firmly at the feet and ripped down the middle by two women walking opposite paths. It seems essential the blood curve symmetrically. The biochemist says: blood is acidic, like vines, simple soil amendment. But a decanted rooster fills maybe two glasses. Only ritual does this. The priestesses wore white, from a distance resembling snow or elision, trailing blood in wind-dust and thirst, until two halves meet and the bird is buried whole. Barely ripe, the pomegranate stains our fingers prying out each humane seed. When we reach the middle we eat the last then lay the joined halves like a deflated ball in the scrub. Avoid improvisation, no god said. Because: how to acquire the eye of a man who died watching hyacinths? Or a hanged godmother's talus? We substitute tea of powdered eyebright and flowering goosefoot. In this way we avoid pesticides, chemical fertilisers, late blight, early frost, neighbours, strays. In June, thunder gifts us new rabbits. By August the grapes flicker like sleeping eyelids and later we'll harvest them delicately with hands braceleted in wasps. How to officiate two acres of future seabed? The source text falters. Inside its missing fragments, static furls like within a seashell. You say: place a cicada on your tongue and wait.

My Wife is an Autumn Leaf

by Jay McKenzie

Highly Commended, Edinburgh Short Story Award 2024

I fall asleep to her feathered breaths, to the rise and fall of her back, then in the morning, she is a leaf. Not just any leaf: specifically a maple leaf in early autumn. Skin that once glistened with dew and sheen and health is now yellow, curling gently at the sides with the beginnings of a brittle crust forming on the very edges of her. There she is, neatly tucked under the duvet, the heat of her body still trapped below in the fibres of the sheet.

Oh, I think. *Oh.*

I carry her downstairs in the palm of my hand, and though I am still in shock, I admire the veins and the midrib, the way they line up exactly with the etchings on the soft side of my hand. *Which is my life line,* I wonder? *And which tells the story of my heart?*

In the kitchen, I lay her on the bench and think about what I should do with her. On the news, they're always debating the merits of setting them free versus trying to preserve them – loud advocates on both sides – but they don't know my wife. I weigh up the merits of putting her in a box. There will be one in our son's room, I'm sure: he always collected little jars and boxes and knicknacks, but I don't want to go in there, not just yet. Besides, a box feels a bit too much like a coffin.

I settle for a ziplock sandwich bag, squeezing out the air to keep the oxygen from further destroying her. The flat, insubstantiality of her little yellow form stilled in plastic is almost too much to bear, and so I sit down by the counter and take a hot, shuddering breath. My eyes slide to the garden, to the weed-choked beds that I just haven't had time for this year. It is ugly out there, ugly and cold and bleak. I wish I'd tended the plants, pulled out the weeds with dirt-specked fingers, but instead I left it to its own devices. *When did I stop noticing the decay?*

In a cafe, my friend greets me with a short hard hug. She blinks through wet eyelashes, because she knows, she understands. Last year, she stood by as her husband became a dandelion. Had to watch as the feathery parachutes were ripped from his head and bits of him were scattered as far as a relentless breeze could carry him. She still has him. He is a withered stalk and a stooped budhead pressed flat between the pages of a weighty sci-fi novel.

Do you have her with you? asks my friend. I push the bag across the table. My friend brings her hand to her mouth. *I'm so sorry,* she whispers.

We sip scalding coffee in silence, neither of us looking at my flat, yellow wife in a bag.

ow long do you think she has left? I ask eventually. My friend bites her lip. *It's okay. You don't have to answer that.*

Steam fogs up the glass and we both watch, transfixed by the plucky droplets that fatten and gather strength enough from each other to make an escape down the window.

Eventually, my friend says, *have you thought about what you are going to do next?*

The words *leaf litter* spring to mind, and I dust them away almost as quickly as I would snowflakes on my shoulder. My wife is not litter. I will not let her become that.

Back home, I set my wife on the windowsill. I boil the kettle and force another hot drink down my throat. It is drier than

I've known it, parched. In the bag, my wife is less vibrant than she was this morning. No longer the yellow of a child's rendering of the sun, she has developed a sulphurous tint, and the brown that was a sugar-dab crust is encroaching further onto her skin.

I want to push open the door to our son's room. To yell, *look what you've done to your mother,* but I freeze on the threshold, my impotent fury from downstairs just a sad wisp of a thing on arrival. *What good would it do anyway?* I think, and take my shaking hand from the doorknob.

At night, I lay my wife on the pillow by my head. I whisper to her in the dark. *Come back to me,* I say. *I am not ready for this.* But she is silent in response.

I'm on the edge of the sleep-abyss when panic drives me to sit up, flick on the bedside lamp. *I'm sorry,* I tell my wife. *What was I thinking?*

I place her in my bedside drawer on top of the journal she bought me whose pages remain as virginal as new snow. I try not to think about my thrashing, restless head crumpling what is left of her.

By morning, my wife is the shade of a turning pear. Tawny bruises rest like thumbprints on her skin.

I thought you'd last longer if I squeezed out the air, I tell her. *What is it that you want?*

In response, she ruffles, though there is no breeze inside the sandwich bag.

I search our history for a time she may have talked about this, but back then, back when we talked, we never could have imagined this happening. Not to us. Not to her.

The books on our shelves offer no help either, though I recall how much she enjoyed The Unlikely Pilgrimage of

Harold Fry and wonder if I've left it too late to press her between words of beautiful agony for a man walking off his grief.

By noon, she is crumpled. To look at, she is the texture of that good leather satchel we packed our boy off to school with. It had belonged to a grandfather or a great uncle or someone covered in the historic dust motes of family stories passed down until nobody can remember the details and who cares because this satchel is a *vintage work of art.*

Remember, I say. *Remember how smart he looked.*

I'm deceived by what look like soft creases on her surface, buffed patches where the skin reflects light. I pull her out of the bag, but her petiole catches on the locking strips and snaps like a forest twig under a hunter's boot.

Oh God! I bring my wife to my lips where they meet the harsh truth of how crisp she has become. *I'm so sorry,* I whisper.

Within the week, she's brittle, falling from her pale frame like the glitter that streamed off our boy's artworks when he carried them home from school in mittened hands. My wife shivers from her stalk, leaving a feather-soft skeleton behind.

She is transparent now. I hold her to the light and see only the gloam of approaching winter behind a map of veins.

I've failed you, I murmur on a cold crisp night that sees a gleam of frost dusting cars and gates and window ledges. *I should have preserved you sooner.* I curse the way I dithered over her books, wasting precious time when I could have been pressing her still-recognisable form between pages.

There's a full moon tonight and everything glows silver and white. I thought I could beg the moon for some help, but his face is blank and unblinking, and I feel ridiculous for even thinking it. There's also a little voice that I keep pushing down that says, *show her the full moon. She may not see another.*

My wife is resting in my hand when a breeze lifts her. She dances for a moment before she's dropped onto a grass verge, brown with the decay of an early winter.

No!

I scan the exposed tree roots, the dirt, the twigs for the ghost of her.

Please, I beg an unseeing moon. *Please,* I ask his deaf ears.

And then I see her.

There's a puddle, a muddy thing that half-hides her from view. If it weren't for the spider-silk lines of her veins, she would have been lost to me forever, buried beneath the coming snow.

I scoop her out, wilting now with the weight of the water, the tip of her gone. My breath is warm against my hands and I blow a hot desert wind onto what is left of her.

My love, I say. *My love my love my love.*

The stairs in our house are mountains. I'm panting by the time I reach the top and have to curl over my wife to catch my breath at our son's bedroom door. I remembered, or perhaps she told me on the hurried journey back home, a book between who's pages she might want to be pressed.

The doorknob is warm, as though a hand held it for a while and has only recently departed. There's a drumming in my chest and the door peels back to reveal the bedroom, smugly preserved in rusts and beiges.

My boots creak on the floorboard, and my voice floats back as though I have tripped back in time. *Are you out of bed?* and that giggle that was syrup and moss and wide fields full of blooming daisies. I keep my eyes on the bookshelf, not permitting myself to look right or left or anywhere in between.

It is bound in blue suede. *Life's too short for a crappy diary,* he said once. I stay standing as I flick through the pages, finding the right words to nestle my wife into while she reclines softly in my palm.

This page, I think. *These words.*

Looping and neat, he guides my finger across the whorls of his thoughts made letters.

The hardest thing, he wrote. *The hardest thing about knowing you are going to die is figuring out when to say goodbye to your parents.*

I lay my wife in the crease between his words, close the book, close my eyes.

Fast Lane

by Fiona Ritchie Walker

Highly Commended, Edinburgh Flash Fiction Award 2024

Andrea offers her friend the damp swimsuit. 'Borrow mine, I'm done. Early meeting today.' Mia takes the low-cut blue and gold. So different from her plain black, forgotten, at home. How long since they shared clothes. University? Andrea always choosing blue. To match her eyes.

Goggles on, Mia swims between tadpole heads, cold frisking her bones. Only Vin in the fast lane. On impulse she follows his white water to the deep.

At the turn, a hand, firm, between her legs. Mia gasps, smiles, draws her husband close. But Vin's eyes can't lie. Behind the goggles, he was expecting blue.

A Day for the Ducks

by David McGrath

Highly Commended, Edinburgh Short Story Award 2024

They woke in each other's arms to begin the Sunday –
naked, estranged – a pair of ducks waking from dreams in
which they were swans.

He grabbed his underpants from the floor and struggled
them on as he ran for the en suite – fast.

She sprang up in search of clothes, stopping all of a sudden
to outstretch her palms to God, asking Him to ease up on
the hangover for ten fucking seconds. She put on a pair of
sweat pants and a cardigan, hid her strapless bra and
thong, draped her dress across the chair and then looked
at her new shoes, found them destroyed with puddle dirt
and the hangover pressing like a dirty, little, rotten, cock-
sucking, bitch. She sat down on the edge of the bed to
collect herself, and looking into the dresser mirror,
someone stared back, someone more on in years than she
remembered, someone who was old.

He had stopped breathing and was making a low, choking
moan over the toilet bowl that ended in a dry retch until up
came the Sambuca, the viscous whiskey, the dark rum
soup, the lager and the alcopops with the fizz still in them.
He looked at himself in the mirror. Someone stared back,
someone older than he remembered, someone who was
fucking old.

When he finally opened the bathroom door there was a
half-naked little girl standing in front of him with a

disgusted expression. She had chubby cheeks and shiny ringlets – Goldilocks in her underwear.

'Were you gettin' sick were ya?' she asked.

'I was, yeah. Yeah, I was. Must've been bad food.'

'Me bollocks,' the little girl said.

'Vanessa, watch your language or you'll get a slap,' said her mother, still sitting on the bed, not quite sure what to do or what to say or how to act.

'But the smell of beer off'm,' Vanessa said then lost interest in the conversation and attempted to balance on her tippy toes. She tumbled and used his arm as support.

'Wow,' he said, feeling dirty and perverse in his Giorgio Armani underpants, a little girl holding him.

'It's called *en pointe*. Ballet. It's hard as fuck.'

'Vanessa, I'm warning you,' she said, head in her hands and looking down at the carpet.

Vanessa began showing him *demi-pliés*. He put both his hands over his groin and then slid one down to try cover his hairy thighs. He brushed past Vanessa to sit on the bed and pull a sheet over his waist.

'Come on, Vanessa, let...' she said and stalled, '*the man* get dressed.'

'Me dress is in your wardrobe,' Vanessa said.

'Jesus, what time is it?' she asked. This was serious. The game had changed. She looked at the alarm clock on the locker then leaned in to make sure it really said the time it said. 'Jesus fucking Christ. It's half ten. Where's your Granny?"

'She went to hers to get ready. We thought you were up.'

'Ah Jesus, get ready now, Vanessa – we'll be late,' she said, grabbing an outfit in dry cleaners' plastic from her wardrobe, stood at the bathroom door for a split second, took a look towards the toilet to make sure it was safe then shut the door. The electric shower powered on.

'So, are you my Daddy now?'

'Daddy? There, eh, see like...'

'Relax, I'm only messin' with ya. Do ya swim?'

'Swim? I do yeah, eh yeah, not very well though.'

'I have to use armbands. Paula Dunne doesn't. She can swim without armbands and won't shut up about it,' Vanessa said, outstretching her arms over her head in two wide arcs, attempting a pirouette. 'Wanna see me dress? It's gorgeous.' Vanessa walked over to the wardrobe, opened the bottom drawer and used it as a step-up. She unhooked a white fluffy ball and threw it onto the bed then tried a *grand jete* down off the drawer, landing badly.

'Mind yourself,' he said.

'I'm grand. Relax,' Vanessa said, picking herself up off the ground.

'You getting married?' he asked, nodding at the big, white, fluffy dress.

'It's me first Holy Communion today. I've to eat Jesus and all that.'

He put his head in his hands and pressed all ten fingers into it hard.

'You look like trampled shite. Don't get sick on my dress or I'll burst ya.'

Vanessa got her dress out of his vomiting radius and laid it on the ground, a chiffon, satin and lace embroidered ball of white floral pattern that materialized in his broken head as some sort of hole in the universe. She stepped inside it, left foot first then the right and pulled it up and around her, vanishing inside the white except for her head.

'Do me zip up will ya?'

She walked over to him, presenting him with her back.

'Eh, well, do you want to wait for your Mammy to do that?'

'Ah would ya stop and go on.'

He took the zip and pulled it up quickly, catching the material in the rung.

'Careful.'

He took it again and poked out the material from the rung, proceeding to pull it up gently, looking away as he did so, ready to leap up and declare his innocence should authorities burst through the door.

'I've a tiara as well. It's gorgeous. Dad has it outside the door. Bring in the tiara, Dad!' Vanessa shouted out to the hallway.

The films were all wrong – life did not flash before your eyes in the final moments. Death did. And it was a violent one where nobody could hear him scream, at the hands of Dad and all of his North Dublin inner-city cronies armed with wrenches and vices and blowtorches and when he begged them to just finish him off they all laughed and singed his eyeballs with cigarettes.

'Relax,' Vanessa said. 'I'm only messin. Where you from, the country?'

'Yes. I'm from Mayo.'

'You have any brothers and sisters?'

'A sister.'

'I have two half-brothers. They're a pair of little cunts.' She affixed her bag over her shoulder and took beaded white gloves out it.

The shower switched off.

'She never takes showers when she's the only one in the house. Isn't that weird? What do you think of veils?'

'Veils?'

'The ones over your face you muppet, that you wear for weddings and maybe Holy Communions. Veils – white veils,' said Vanessa attempting another *demi-plié* in the dress.

'What do *you* think of them?'

'Hate them,' she said and palmed down the bodice, reached her head back as far as she could manage so as to make sure everything was in order. 'Rotten things they are. It's a Communion. What do you need a veil for?'

'Does Paula Dunne have a veil?'

'She won't shut up about it.'

'Tiaras are the way forward I think,' he said. 'In my opinion. To hell with veils.'

Vanessa took her eyes off him for a split second and he pulled up his trousers underneath the sheet. She heard the movement and turned back around, staring unashamedly, trying to catch one last glimpse of his zigzagged underpants. He pulled out the bit of sheet that had been tucked inside his trousers with the maneuver, stood up and swayed a tad from the blood rush to the head. He found his t-shirt and put it on, his shoes then put them on. The socks were abandoned.

'What's your job?'

'I'm a sparky. I wire houses and factories for electricity, make sure it all has power and lights and all that sort of thing. Yeah – electrician.'

'You make much dosh?'

'Not these days. Work's a bit scarce actually,' he said and waited for her to ask another question but she did not. Instead she tucked her bottom lip beneath the top one, folded her arms at the same time, her heel the only part of her right foot that touched the carpet.

'Right, right, Communion,' he said and reached for his wallet in his back pocket. He found a twenty and a fiver. It was the last bit of money he had until Thursday's dole. He pinched the fiver inside the wallet and looked at her looking at the notes. He took out the twenty and gave it over.

'Cheers,' she said, slipping it inside her bag. 'What about the five?'

'You want the five, too?'

'What do you need it for?'

He handed over the five, too. She slipped it inside her bag with the twenty.

'You want the wallet and all?' he asked.

'No. I've a purse.'

The bathroom door opened and she came out dressed in a coral pants suit and white blouse, her hair cleaned, her face scrubbed, teeth brushed and rinsed twice with mouthwash. She looked rejuvenated and put a spring in her step to show it, to show she was rushed, to show he had to skedaddle. She plugged in the hairdryer and began shaking it, running it through wet strands of her hair.

'Vanessa, are you ready?'

'I've to put my socks and shoes on.'

'Well go do it will you, or we'll be late.'

Vanessa went to her room. He stood up and shifted weight from one foot to the other. She looked at him in the reflection of the dresser's mirror and shook the hairdryer harder through her hair.

'I'll head off, get out of your way,' he said.

'OK,' she said. 'Any of the buses at the end of the road will take you into town.'

'Brilliant. Good luck with it.'

'What?' she said, the noise of the dryer getting the better of the conversation. She switched it off and turned around to look at him, making sure not to smile but not to frown either. Neutral, keeping it neutral.

'I just said – good luck with the Communion. She's a nice kid. She's funny.'

'Thanks,' she said. 'If I could stop her swearing.'

'It's a phase with them, isn't it?' he said. He was doing well. Mature, like.

'She's just doing it to get noticed.'

'Well, I think you have the next big ballerina on your hands there. I'll be watching out for her.'

'Right. Yea,' she said, turning back around.

'No, it's just that I'm off to Canada soon. Toronto.'

'I remember you saying,' she said.

'No, I meant,' he said and stopped. She watched him raise his hand to behind his ear like he was about to ask a question in school but not quite sure whether it was a stupid one or not. He took a step to her, outstretched a hand, made to say something and decided against it.

'Bye,' he said finally, his eyes opened hard, suggesting she could maybe say something instead.

'Bye now,' she said, switching the hairdryer back on and getting to work on the strands still wet. He turned. She got on with drying. He hurried down the stairs and opened the front door then closed it behind him. The rain had started and the puddles collected. Drops dripped from the locked bicycles and that was it really. A day for the ducks. The houses snoozed on, curtains still drawn. The cars stayed parked, nobody to work, nobody for a jog, nobody venturing out for fresh orange juice or breakfast rolls, nobody even able to look at food, a time fit for only paracetemol and maybe a hammer over the head to knock them out until Monday. He looked up at the bedroom window.

'It'll be fine,' Vanessa said out through the letterbox.

'Thanks,' he said.

'You want a loan of some money?'

'No,' he said. 'I'll be alright.'

Back to life

by Honor Somerset

Highly Commended, Edinburgh Flash Fiction Award 2024

There was liver in the fridge. Susanna's liver. Not a crime scene, just that Susanna seemed to have fallen apart. Or rather her life had so fallen apart that her body had too, leaving parts of her scattered around the house. A heart in the bedroom, a stomach in the study, a couple of kidneys in the bathroom.

Somehow her legs were still walking, lost, going in one direction, then another, bumping into walls. The mechanics were there – some of them, at least – but no whole. No backbone, her spirit slumped in the corner, motionless.

A pile of post, not a cat on the mat, but post on the flat, wiry matting, gathering dust.

Outside, a whistle of wind and a scuffle. A shriek, a yowl and a bundle of fur crashed through the cat-flap, coming up short against a chair leg. In the distance, the scream of a fox receded.

A tongue licked a paw, washed a small ear, which flicked, alert. A nose twitched, and four paws went exploring. Chased Susanna's legs and scratched them to a halt. A paw poked the slumpy mess in the corner: move. From under the sofa another paw yanked out a spine and a nose nudged Susanna's hand: feed me. Her fingers caressed the furry head which leapt away: feed me. And she followed, gathering herself together, into the kitchen.

Later, in the bedroom, her hand shot to her chest, surprised to find a heart, once more, beating.

The Rowan

by Fiona Donn

Highly Commended, Edinburgh Short Story Award 2024

I have a story to tell and I long for someone to hear it. The wind, blowing hard off the Atlantic, is cold today, and I fight against it. The sky is a darkening bruise of blue and black above me, and the cows, knowing heavy rain will soon fall, have meandered down off the hill and are sheltering under the canopy of alder and ash at the edge of the glebe. I call out louder than I have ever managed before, a sudden outburst borne of frustration rather than necessity, but there is no-one to listen and the wind quickly snatches and carries it away, as if it had never happened at all.

Sometimes I wonder if the gusts could carry the sound of me miles inland, over the desolate muddy tracks and narrow whin-lined roads to the nearest village. I imagine it arriving, startling the recipients with its sudden disquieting lament, alerting them to my distress call. Fat, wet drops start to strike me with force, and using the old rowan for shelter, I sit and wait.

I can still see her, what's left of her, down in the ditch. For a while she stared back at me, but then the crows came and now she sees nothing at all; reduced to a mess of cloth and bone with grasses and wildflowers growing through and over. How I had battled those crows, fiercely attacking until I grew tired. Eventually I had retreated, their stubborn determination greater than my threat, despite my bigger size. Others were drawn silently and unseen in the night by the tempting odour, frantically picking and gnawing at whatever they could with their ripping teeth. I was defeated by them all, I could no more protect her now than when she was living.

On dark days like this, when it's impossible to tell where the vast grey ocean beyond ends and the sky begins, I anchor myself in the swaying branches and try to remember the before. The rowan dutifully stands guard in the garden at the rear of the cottage, the cottage itself offering some protection from the strong westerly winds that blow in and bend the branches of more exposed trees until they stay that way – crooked and bent. On clear, calm days I could sit on the red tin roof and watch them both tending the croft. They each had their own jobs it seemed, him mending, sawing, digging, planting – her milking cows, feeding hens and collecting eggs. They had a rhythm and harmony like the waves washing over the pebbles on the shore. Once or twice, I got to the rabbit in his trap before he did. He ran at me, shouting with fury, but I was quick to take off, narrowly missing a swift kick from his leather boot. She shook her head and laughed at his futile outburst, and hands on hips, cursing lightly, he tossed his head back and laughed too. He left around two full moons later, and all the jobs after that belonged to her. The steady rhythm of the place fell out of step and I knew to leave the rabbits from then on, she would need them.

In the time that he had been gone, we had become friends, her and I. Leaving scraps for me on the stone wall surrounding the cottage, she would wait inside and watch for me swooping down and hungrily devouring every morsel, smiling encouragingly at me as I did so. I was grateful, and as the seasons turned, I trusted her enough to let her sit nearby. She would speak softly to me, lonely I suppose, not minding that I regarded her in silence. I brought her gifts in return, sometimes berries, or a pretty, washed-smooth shard of sea glass from the shore. How she delighted in these offerings, scooping them up and examining them as if rare treasures, a wide smile spreading across her face and eyes darting from the rowan to the bracken and heather-strewn hills beyond to see if she could spot me. She was glad of me back then, in the dismal solitude of his absence, and I of her. We had an understanding beyond the scraps and gifts, something deeper, more meaningful and enduring.

He had been gone for many seasons. The rowan's branches had sagged with the weight of plump, juicy berries several times over and the geese had come and gone.

I watched him jump off the mail cart at the end of the road the day he returned, wincing as his boots hit the hard-frosted ground. Bent slightly under the weight of the canvas bag over his shoulder, his green uniform caked heavily with dried mud, he stood staring at the stone cottage in the distance. Thick smoke from the chimney betrayed the fire in the hearth, and washing pegged on a single line outside flapped horizontal in the crisp breeze. For a moment he closed his eyes, the only movement his dark hair whipping silently in the salty wind. The screeching of a gull broke his reverie, and hesitating slightly, he began the final heavy steps of his journey home.

The cottage door had flung open and she had run wet-cheeked to him, throwing her arms around him with force. Laughing between sobs, she eventually let go and led him by the hand inside. I watched with interest from my favourite branch in the rowan as she placed the tin bath in front of the fire that night, painstakingly filling it one kettle at a time. Tenderly, she let the warm water slip over him, gently washing every broken piece of him as he sat weary and motionless. Puffing my night-black feathers for warmth and bowing my head to sleep, I became aware of more sobbing, ragged and raw, and this time his.

I can feel when there's a storm coming. The air becomes still, as if the sky has forgotten how to breathe, and there's an unsettling prickly feeling that won't let me be. I would normally leave, find a hollow somewhere and wait it out, but something that day made me stay. I had seen little of her in the time since his return; fleeting moments when she left the cottage to fill a basket from the peat stack, or pull vegetables from the garden. That day, the day of the storm, heaving a full basket back from the stack, she paused and scanned the horizon. Her golden hair appearing copper in the orange glow of near night, her eyes narrowed and brow furrowed in concentration, she was looking for me. In my unease I had moved far from my usual places and was a good deal harder to find. I flapped my wings and called out to her. She understood. "I'm still here," I said. Satisfied, she returned inside, gently closing the door behind her. I felt a pull to her, and immediately returned to the rowan, choosing a low, thick branch. I pressed close against the trunk for protection and braced myself for what was to come.

The first flash startled me, in the blackness of night everything just for a moment had become brighter than a clear summer morning. I had little time to recover when a long, low, deafening growl boomed hard across the sky, calling for submission. Distracted briefly from my own fear, I became aware of terror-stricken shouting from the cottage. Shouting first and then screams, one shrill and piercing, and then another. With no lamps burning inside I could not see in the window. Another flash – brilliant as day, lighting up the whole glen. A fleeting glance of his hand on her neck, squeezing hard, blood running fast from a deep gash on her forehead. Darkness. My eyes needing time to adjust, took a moment or two to make sense of everything, but I could make out a dark shape moving away from the cottage, stumbling. She was weaving a path not straight, but instead faltering in all directions. Another long, booming growl. A small high-pitched sound escaped from her and she took a few more misplaced, staggered steps. Panic rose in me and I swooped down to a fence post nearby her shadowy form. Clumsily, she turned to face me and I saw a glimpse of recognition in her eyes, just a flicker of familiarity, before she swayed several more small, unbalanced steps and fell backwards... down.

I stayed there a while, beside her unmoving body, waiting for her to show a sign of being something more. Despite the sudden rain, I would not leave until it drummed forcefully on the ground, compelling me to retreat to the rowan and keep watch from there. No sooner had I settled when came another flash, accompanied by a loud, swift bang; this time from inside the cottage, as if all the lamps had been lit at once for the briefest moment. The storm was finally at an end but I would not settle to sleep that night, nor the next, my unease was too great and my spirit too low.

It is lonely here for me now. Perhaps the mail cart will return soon and with it someone to pay heed to me. Such fuss I will make over by the ditch and cry, "Look, here she is!" Gently, she will be rolled in a blanket and taken quietly away on that creaking cart to somewhere with daffodils in the spring and roses in the summer. Him too I suppose, wiped clean and in his uniform. They will sing for them, as they have for so many before, but his name will not be carved with the others.

The rain has eased now and the cows are on the move again, grazing as they go. The clusters of haws on the hawthorn are almost gone and the whins have started to bloom yellow. In time the blaeberries will be out and I will eat my fill of those, if the grouse and pheasant don't gorge them ahead of me. I will leave one day soon, carving a path through the fresh breeze over purple clad hills and shimmering lochs, but I am not yet ready. For now, you will find me here waiting, in this steadfast old rowan, and I have a story to tell.

All That Remains

by Denarii Peters

Highly Commended, Edinburgh Flash Fiction Award 2024

I am temptation, an illicit thrill, the old witch's last and greatest creation. Come closer. See how I sparkle. Iridescent green, purple, blue... Inside this tiny bottle I could be a dragon held suspended or merely oil on water.

That's right. Take me in your hand. Hold me to your eye. What do you see? Floating fragments of precious metals, crushed rubies and emeralds, all of them changing, flowing, coalescing...

What am I? What did she bring into being with her mixture of blood and herbs gathered on a cold midnight beneath the full moon? Could I bind your lover or destroy your enemies? Will I bring you wealth or end all your hopes?

There is only one way to find out and that is not to replace me on the high, dusty shelf for another to discover.

You came in here to seek anything she might have left behind, bringing with you the reek of her burning flesh. You would have been her apprentice if she had let you. So yes, you could be right. I may be meant for you alone.

I am all the magic that remains in this place. There are no incantations for you to take away, no books in a sealed chest. She never did learn to write.

So what am I? Her final gift or her final curse? It all depends on what she knew, on whether or not she guessed the one who betrayed her...

...was you.

Hen Night with Mermaids

by Lindsay Gillespie

Shortlisted, Write Mango Short Story Award 2024
Longlisted, Edinburgh Short Story Award 2024

Sea-mist wraps the pier in a veil of fishnet and floats on in with the evening tide. The tide has washed up something else. A couple of mermaids. Tonight their plan is to get legless on Brighton beach. The biggest mermaid, Fortuna, flexes her webbed fingers and crunches up the last Heineken in her fist. Maria Assumpta, the littlest one, and the drunkest one, is face-planted in the shingle.

'Home now,' she goes.

Fortuna flicks her tongue from side to side to lick the evening air.

'I'm getting short-fin mako,' she says, 'come on, I'm starving.'

She pings the pebbledash from Maria Assumpta's cheek and yanks her up onto her tail.

'Remember what we're here for tonight. Elaunia, do us all a favour and stick a smile on,' she says.

Elaunia, mermaid number three, has been in a moody the whole swim in. It's her first time tonight, and she's not exactly hiding her nerves.

'It's off-putting, okay,' Fortuna tells her, 'it will put the lads right off.'

'I need a smoke.'

'After supper.'

TGI Fryday's, bang opposite the beach, is rammed. Open all night, every night, it's where the clubbers, stags and the hens traditionally finish their night. Take a typical Friday night, because here we are on a typical Friday night; it's wrecked tiaras and Hawaiian hula girls from Hastings. The Spice Girls are still big – Sporty Spice is easy: a trackie shrunk in the wash, and a scraped-back ponytail. But by the time they get to Fryday's it's tricky to say who's who – everyone's wrecked. No-one looks like the person they started the night as. Glitter stuck on teeth, and splintered fingernails. The hens are thinking of only one thing now, or two things to finish the night off. Fish and chips. And copping off.

Mostly chips though.

Shane and Marvin jiggle in the queue amongst the coconut shell bras.

'It's a Bounty advert! And the only blokes here,' goggles Shane 'are you and me.'

There is another bloke. Only he's behind the counter. His job is to splat the slabs of fish down in the shining fat, then tow them out in their little frilled coats of batter. He has a greaser's long ponytail wriggling out of his paper mob-cap.

He doesn't count.

The Mermaids barge in. By-pass the queue. The big one, Fortuna, bellies straight up to the counter.

'Oy, Ariel... you blind? There's a queue here,' says Shane.

Fortuna goes right ahead and orders.

'Three chips please.'

'Fish?' asks the fryer.

The mermaid sniffs, 'Fresh?'

The fish fryer points his fishslice at the blackboard.

'Codplaicehaddockwhitingcurrysaucepeas. And dogfish.'
There's always dogfish. He's never sold a dogfish. It could
do with a rebrand, a fancier name.

'Dogfish,' the mermaids look at one another, 'and we'll have
it how it comes, out the fridge.'

The frying bloke steps back and considers the mermaids
on the other side of his counter.

'Raw?' he says.

'Raw.' The three mermaids nod.

Shane steps up to the counter. He has one arm around a
Mother of the Bride, and the other is around Lady Gaga.

'This is a queue. And these ladies happen to be in front of
you.'

He gestures at the pink-eyed hens. Though Marvin swears
it wasn't him, someone starts it, and someone amps it up.

'Fightfightfight!'

It's turning into a proper Friday night out. Marvin is always
up for a bit of a fight. A chip fight would do.

'Ladies and gents,' says the fish-fryer. That's all he says. He
picks up the salt-shakers and starts to shakes them like
maracas, to change the tone, lighten the mood.

'Salt? Vinegar? Say when.'

But Elaunia, the middle-sized mermaid, doesn't say when.
She likes watching the juggling fish-fryer. Fortuna turns to
the boys and the pissed hens.

'Eat first, fighting after,' she says.

Maria Assumpta fingercombs her aqua ringlets. She leans
over the counter and says to the fish-fryer: 'Your dogfish is
cat-shark. Actually.'

The fish-fryer thinks they're the best mermaid hens he's ever seen. Especially the littlest one – her skin white as cigarette paper, her lips lustrous and ketchupy. And her smell. The shop stinks of it. The sudden reek of what the high tide leaves behind after a winter storm.

The mermaids leave and drift down onto the black beach to eat their chips.

Marv stares at them wobbling out of the door. They're legless.

Sporty Spice and Lady Gaga poke Shane and Marv.

'You said you were going to tell them. Barging in, cutting in. Freaks.'

'I will. I am. Stay here a minute and look after my chips.'

Shane plunges onto the beach.

Marv follows.

Down by the groynes the mermaids aren't eating their chips. Too hot.

'Blow on them like this. Those girls in the shop, with the legs, that's what they do.'

Maria Assumpta turns around, 'Those lads. They're coming. I'm definitely going to chuck up for real.'

Fortuna digs her nails in and scrams Maria Assumpta's cheek.

'Don't you dare. Tonight is hard enough as it is. Make like you're having fun, hahaha. You're so not coming next year.'

The beach stones chink like glass as the boys lumber and lurch.

'Hey, mermaids! Okay if we join? Swap you vodka for some chips? We left ours back there.'

Fortuna, mistress of ceremonies, nods and takes a swig of warm vodka. If all goes to plan, like other years, they could get the job done in ten, fifteen minutes, and be home by daybreak.

Marv moves in closer to Maria Assumpta, and she passes him a chip. 'You'll never guess,' he says, 'but I've got a tattoo of you. On my bum. Wanna see?'

He's fiddling with his belt when a seagull bombs him.

He flaps at the bird, 'You can piss off.'

When the bird bombs them again, Elaunia moves quick. She shakes out her green hair like a fishing net and traps it.

Nips the head off.

She chews a mouthful, 'Boney. I always forget they're just grease and wattle.' She makes a throttling noise, and coughs up some beak.

The boys stop laughing.

The tide is coming in faster and faster.

Here we go, thinks Fortuna, it's time.

 Her silver eyes shiver.

'Fancy a swim?' She fixes a look at Elaunia and Maria Assumpta. She needs them to pick up on what she's doing.

She finds Shane's fingers and pulls him down to the water's edge, where the froth is whipped like spit and the waves are sucking on the stones. He twists off her scallop shell bra.

'Follow,' she says.

She slides beneath the first wave. The boy is lost already. He can't see her, can't hear her. He smashes and kicks out at the sea. She calls him, he changes direction, he tries to find the muscle of the waves to go with that. But the sea won't let him. He's further out than he's ever been, swimming towards the moon, swimming against the tide. Now he is past the end of the pier, close to the wind farm, with its stiff little arms pointing the way back to shore. He looks back to where he thinks the beach might be.

'Marv!'

Marv must be behind him, yes, Marv is catching up with him.

It's not Marv. The other mermaids are on him. They catch him.

Mermaid sex is hard and punishing. Their nails – like broken mussel shells – shred him, their tongues thick and long as an octopus' arm push down his throat. They choke him, take turns to empty him. The biggest mermaid raises her head, opens her jaw of blackened shark teeth and bites his throat. It's over. They're done.

The mermaids lay their egg cases down amongst the sea gardens, and in the caves where the snake-lock anenomes live. The bigger eggs they weave amongst the gutweed closer to shore. Those are the ones you most often come across, that wash up after a storm. If you find one, best to put it back, and let the next tide take it back.

Three early morning fishermen out for summer mackerel find the boy. They haul him out, he is the colour of malt vinegar. Do you know how lucky you are, they say. That we turned back. The wind is all weirded up, and something was spooking the catch. Then we found you. By the trench. All the wrecks are down there, in the trench, and the dead men. The first one, the Fortuna, she went down in 1897, the Maria Assumpta went just after the war. And the last one. The last one was the Elaunia. The last of the shipwrecks.

Language of the birds

by MJ Burns

Shortlisted, Edinburgh Flash Fiction Award 2024

My wee baby in her buggy. The trees by Loch Shin wave to her, summer-heavy and whispering. Across her shining eyes, their reflections roll. She screeches and startles pigeons. Flapping, whistling flurry. Her smile lights up my heart like the surface of the loch in the sun. My baby begins to sing. Beautiful tiny voice – music wordless as the birds.

To summon a song in return, I breathe in the air of my home, heady with the smell of the earth. An ancestral tug in my soul – I should be able to sing to her in Gaelic.

Gàidhlig

Instead, I bumble through *Old MacDonald Had a Farm*. The music of the whole world in my pocket yet lacking the songs I ought to know. The air around me thrums with centuries of them, but I can hear none of it.

In another life I'd know

Cainnt nan Eun,

the Language of the Birds. Known to make them draw near and listen. I could have taught her to talk to the pigeons in the trees.

Gur thu, gur thu, gur thu

Chan ann de mo chuideachd thu

In this life, I heard the song on TikTok. I feel the ache of passing the custody of our traditions to the scholars, the hobbyists, the Outlander fans, the museums where scratchy recordings project a Highland world in grayscale. I have no songs to pass down to my baby. She, as I, will learn her heritage from tea towels, tourist shops and Duolingo's owl.

Gypsy

by Kerry Anderson

Shortlisted, Edinburgh Flash Fiction Award 2024

A vibration penetrates the pen's baked earth floor. A grey muzzle lifts between splayed paws. Eyes search but cannot penetrate a cloudy haze.

Routine has formed Gypsy's life. Learning her craft under the guidance of older collies until it was her turn to lead, casting wide to gather the mob in the flat golden paddocks. Every year a joy until the younger dogs left her floundering in their dust and she couldn't jump up on to the ute tray. One morning she was left behind in her pen. And then the next.

Footsteps at this time of the day are unusual.

A familiar scent reaches her nostrils, then a soft hand on her head. Propping herself up on stiffened front legs she wills the hind ones to follow. Gentle hands encircle bony ribs pulling her upright. The indignity of a clip being attached to her collar.

As if she wouldn't follow.

Stumbling she falls into step at his side. Slowly they navigate past the familiar stand of eucalypts. Nostrils twitch in anticipation as they pass the shearing shed. Nothing. No work today.

A pause to open the gate and they walk on. In her memory she knows exactly where they are in the back paddock. A cool breeze ruffles her coat. Winter is coming.

He sits beneath the big gum, and gratefully she lowers her tired body and rests her grey muzzle on his warm thigh. A hand gently caresses her tattered ears.

Together, they sit one last time.

Blue Juice

by Abhainn Connolly

Longlisted, Edinburgh Short Story Award 2024

A catch pole is a lightweight, plastic-coated cable that is one point five to two metres long. There is a loop at one end that can be tightened or loosened by a rotating handle at the other. They are designed to safely restrain and control animals by tightening a noose over their neck, allowing you to keep a safe distance from a stray or dangerous dog.

When first using one, you are clumsy. In training, you practise on stuffed animals in the giant loading bay of the animal shelter. There's a large countertop to your right with vaccination supplies, a hand-and-eye-washing station, and tiny traps and cages now empty of their former neighbourhood menaces. To the left are massive kennels with heavy-duty wires that are three metres tall, with chain-link roofs. This, you now know, is your safety net. The goal is to take the aggressive street dogs that come in from the truck, loop the catch pole around their neck, and then manage to drag and shove them into the kennels and lock the door without being mauled, even while they are lunging and bucking and rolling, dead set on making you pay for the trial they are suffering.

Your new appendage seems to have a mind of its own. You accidentally whack a colleague in the bum when you turn to listen to their instructions. You tighten the noose too little, and a rambunctious cotton giraffe escapes your keen manoeuvring. But eventually, you learn how gravity interacts with the distance. You see how you can control an animal twenty kilos heavier than you by holding it at the right angle, how the space gives you power, leverage. You learn that too tight is always better than too loose. You cage a giant teddy bear in three seconds flat. You are ready, at least physically, to encounter your first feral dog.

The stakes are always high. You will either be alone, or you will have everyone in the loading bay's lives in your hands. These dogs are brought in because they have *already* bitten or mauled someone. They never get a trial – when dogs bite, they are immediately sentenced. You come to realise, years later, that they are, rightfully or not, indignant for this treatment. No matter how well you care for them in the ten days they spend with you, they know they are looking into the eyes of their executioner.

Every day, when I went to feed Hank, I would load his bowl with extra chicken, little treats, yoghurt – anything nice that was donated that week. I would walk by his kennel a few extra times a day to try and toss in some meat. I still believed, at that point in my life, that everyone and everything could be rehabilitated with enough love, strategy, and time. I didn't work at the animal shelter because I agreed with the way we did things. My rationale was that maybe I could change it from the inside, and if anyone had to euthanize healthy animals, it should be someone whose heart broke every time they did it, who would treat them with the type of human kindness they hadn't yet experienced in their life.

Hank was a whopping eighty kilos. He would jump on the front of the kennel when we passed or approached, snapping, snarling, and barking. The door would rattle and I'd always double check the locks. I'd have to take paper towels and wipe a bubbly froth from the front of my scrubs after visiting him. It was dangerous just to feed him – once, a volunteer, starry-eyed and well-meaning, heard his fate and tried to slip a secret extra bowl to him before we left for the night, and he caught hold of her finger through the fencing.

I'd been at the animal shelter for over a year. In that time, the "code red" dogs had become my sole responsibility. I was a natural with the catch pole and got accolades for my bedside manner. For as long as I can remember, I've always become calm, decisive, and confident in the face of crisis. We were meant to rotate euthanasia shifts, each person taking on the list on their assigned day. But when I would see a bereaved coworker's demeanour on the morning they were assigned, I would offer to take their shift. I had seen too many people lose their composure in their grief while administering the intravenous medications, and any error in the process could cause suffering in the animal's final moments. Why force my friends and the animals to go through this when my own response was an efficient calm? People started proactively asking me to take their duty. Eventually, I never got a day off from it.

I didn't take into consideration, until it was too late, that my heart was a single heart. That my calm was just as much a maladaptive response to wrongness as those who ran, who broke down sobbing, or whose hands shook so much they couldn't operate the tools needed for the job. That some things, once broken or wild, remain that way.

A syringe pole is six metres long and made of aluminium. Thumb trigger syringe poles operate just like a syringe you find at the doctors' office, except they give you much greater reach. You can gently push the needle into the animal and control the injection from the thumb-operated trigger at the opposite end, and there is no additional pressure on the animal during the injection.

Hank won't stop trying to attack you, even after you inject him with a tranquilliser meant to calm him before you give him the euthanasia drug. You keep missing his thigh, as you are trying to administer it from seven metres away and through a fence, so shots are going in the wrong place on his body and failing to enter his system properly. You have him on a catch pole in your left hand and are trying to aim the syringe pole with the right. For the first time, your own body is shaking. It gets worse every time you miss, and he lunges for you yet again. You must reload another syringe, while still controlling him with your left hand. You are not calm or collected. The door is unlocked and slightly ajar. You nearly tranquilise yourself trying to get the new needle into the pole.

On the third injection, he falls to the ground in the corner of the kennel, mouth open, tongue hanging out the side. His eyes are still open and follow you as you struggle to open the door, walk through the kennel, and seat yourself next to him. His breathing is calming down, though still laboured. You are afraid he will get a new burst of energy and you will meet your end here, but you are practised in this. You move on autopilot.

After a few moments, you hesitantly reach out your hand to pet his forehead. You know, from his intake forms, that he has never been pet by a human before this moment. He looks at you, and his eyes are no longer angry or frantic. They are wide, glassy orbs. You begin to rub his forehead with your thumb, and he squints softly. It surprises you – he enjoys it. You move your hand along in gentle strokes. His ears are the softest things you have ever touched. You notice a sensation on your chest. The front collar of your shirt is soaked. You are crying, big balloons of tears one after the other, a torrent. You notice you have been talking to him. You are sorry. So sorry. So sorry. You love him. It isn't his fault. Of all the options available to you, this is the kindest. You try to interpret the situation for him and fail. You begin to explain the rest of the procedure.

You are going to load up a bright blue liquid into a new syringe. The size of the syringe feels intimate in your hand – it is so small, you two will be so close. You are going to find the most beautiful, big vein on the inside of his thigh. You're going to swab it, sterilise it, and then begin the injection. You tell him you will inject it slowly so that he doesn't have a seizure. That is the biggest mistake beginners make, you explain, as they are hoping to get the whole thing over with, but you tell him that you will not run from him. You tell him that when you are done, you will come grab his head and place it in your lap. You will knead the big muscles in his neck, something you now know he likes. You will tell him he is a good boy. And when his final breath sputters out of him, you will hold him until a supervisor stumbles upon you both, cold and in puddles in the back of the kennel.

'Please Take Care of This Water Bear'

by Joyce Meggett

Shortlisted, Edinburgh Flash Fiction Award 2024

September 3, 2035

Dear Edward James Young,

I am writing to tell you that my tardigrade Stephen lives in a fishbowl that you will find among my things. You'll probably also find a magnifying glass, which you will need to see him, but if not Dad keeps his in the bottom left drawer of his desk.

Tardigrades don't need anything besides damp moss to keep them happy and if the moss dries out they know how to dry out too and wait patiently until they get water again. They can wait for up to thirty years, but you'll be reading this note long before then.

My parents have faithfully promised to keep all my belongings safe. They've already laid in a big supply of cardboard boxes. I can't imagine what I'm going to be like six years from now. A lot like Dad, I expect. Mum once let slip they might not have had me at all if someone hadn't discovered how to let twelve-year-olds sleep right through adolescence. I was starting to get stroppy with Dad so it's definitely time.

Anyway, Stephen will be waiting for me, but just in case I'm the sort of grown-up who doesn't think about microfauna, please find his bowl and sprinkle a bit of water on his moss so he can go back to enjoying life. I know you'll probably be really busy, but I would appreciate it.

Good luck.

Your friend,

Eddie

Husband Marketplace.com
MALE ORDER TODAY

by Claire Marsh
Shortlisted, Edinburgh Flash Fiction Award 2024

Hi, first time poster, looking for advice. Got my Husband in 2008. An old, 1.0 model. From reading the forum posts, I could get way more functionality. Does anyone have a recent, upgraded model I could try for a week? Promise to return it spotless.

Mine's been durable enough. Selecting this model wasn't a mistake. Back then, my expectations were lower. Broke and in my twenties, a model with one previous owner and no bells and whistles did the job.

Over time, my needs have exceeded its operating system's capabilities. There is still some use left. The extension pack I installed helped; now it takes washing out as well as putting it in, makes lunch too (on weekends). But there's no extending its memory. Try and the system crashes. It takes hours, sometimes days, rebooting. Noisily!

The choice available in Husband 2.0 models is astounding. Websites bursting with product images, descriptions, reviews. Swipe right and you can compare them. A few clicks and you're face-to-face, user-testing.

But all the horror stories, wow! Stolen goods, redirected from their legal owners. And flashy, high-end ones only good for a handful of quick uses, incapable of sustaining heavy, everyday application. One woman's arrived half the height, twice the width of its description. Another, said the image online was ten years old, before use and damage.

Any tips welcome. DM me, if you want to make an offer on my Husband 1.0. Sorry, this is limited to my postcode (it's heavy and awkward to haul).

Hilda & Albert

by Chris d'Lacey

Longlisted, Edinburgh Short Story Award 2024

The first time Albert came to the house was the day they started digging up the road. Hilda remembered receiving the letter; Rosemary had read it out for her. Something to do with the gas supply. A man might pop round to talk about it, that's what Rosemary had said.

So when Hilda heard the toilet flush, she thought, at first, it must be them: the gas people. Luckily, she'd just finished pulling on her stockings and had managed to get her feet into her slippers. Her hair needed brushing, but it would have to do.

Pushing hard, she got herself off the bed, picked up her stick and shuffled to the door. There he was, across the landing, coming out of the loo with a newspaper tucked underneath one arm.

"Morning," he said. He sounded gruff, a little northern. He was a big chap, too. A working man. "Expect you know your loo roll holder's bust?"

Hilda did know. It was a nuisance, that thing. The nail for the holder was loose in the wall; the loo rolls were always ending up on the floor.

"It's in the wrong place as well," said the man. "Too far back. You should look at that."

Hilda had, many times. But how was she to fix nails with *her* hands? She'd mention it to Stephen when he came with the shopping. Stephen knew what to do about nails.

"Who are you?" she said, a tremor in her voice. He didn't look like a gas man. He didn't wear one of those bright yellow jackets or hard orange hats. He didn't carry a clipboard. And he didn't smell of gas. He reminded her a little of her father, Eric, who always wore a waistcoat and turned-up trousers.

"I'm Albert," he said.

Hilda leaned on her stick. "How did you get in?"

"Front door were open. You want to lock that at night."

Hilda thought she had. It was part of her routine. Like changing the calendar. And taking her tablets. And filling her pinafore pocket with everything she needed *before* she climbed the stairs. "Who said you could use my toilet?"

"Called up," he said, putting a pipe to his mouth. "Expect you didn't hear."

That was possible. One of Hilda's hearing aids was whistling again. All the same, it wasn't right that this man should have entered her house and used her toilet, uninvited. And he shouldn't be lighting a pipe.

"Stop that," she said, frowning at him. "You'll have this silly thing going off." She pointed her stick at a smoke alarm.

"I wouldn't worry about that," said Albert.

But Hilda did worry. What an embarrassment it had been, the firemen coming that time she'd burnt the toast. An engine outside, blocking the Crescent. The neighbours talking. Mr Walton complaining, because he couldn't move his car. People saying she was a danger to herself. Thank goodness the firemen were friendly. They told her not to worry about Mr Walton, but advised her not to use the grill in future. Too easy to forget about a grill, they said, especially when she'd gone to answer the phone.

"I'll be off, then," said Albert, sucking on his pipe. He waggled a match to put the flame out. "I'll be seeing you again, I expect."

"You won't," said Hilda as he started down the stairs, trailing that awful pipe smoke behind him. That would linger, that would. She'd be smelling that all day. "You've got a nerve. I should report you."

"Aye," he said. And that was him gone.

Later that morning, when Rosemary came in to do a spot of housework, Hilda mentioned Albert's visit.

"Goodness, what a cheek," Rosemary said, with a chuckle. She often chuckled at the things Hilda told her. She flicked a duster over the mantelpiece. "I hope he opened the window afterwards."

Hilda hoped so, too. That pipe smoke was still on the stairs. She was surprised Rosemary hadn't noticed it.

"I've done you some lunch, it's in the fridge," Rosemary said, bustling past on her way to the kitchen. "I've hoovered all round. Shall I feed the birds, too?"

Hilda said bless you. She liked the birds. It was a good idea of Stephen's, putting the feeder by the window where she could watch the birds from the comfort of her chair. The dogs on the Green were too far away now. Some days she fancied she could hear them barking, even if Stephen said she couldn't. She missed seeing the dogs, running and chasing. But the birds kept her company, until she fell asleep.

"So was he nice, this Albert?" Rosemary was back with a bag of seed.

"Ooh, no," said Hilda, sitting up straight. "He was rough. He thought a lot of himself."

Rosemary smiled and unlocked the patio door. "Some folk are like that," she said, almost whispering. "Have you seen those boys again lately?"

Oh, they were a trial, those boys, always knocking things over or moving things about. The saucepan in the airing cupboard, that was them. And it was definitely them who'd hidden the underwear. The lady on the phone had said it wasn't an emergency, not being able to find your knickers. But how could Hilda get dressed without knickers? It was all very well Stephen shouting at her, he didn't have children running round the house.

Rosemary didn't wait for an answer. She stepped outside and topped up the feeder. When she came back in, it was time for her to leave. "If that Albert comes again, you tell him to buzz off."

Hilda squared her shoulders. "I shall press my button."

Rosemary leaned forward and tidied the cord around Hilda's neck. "I don't think that will be necessary, Hilda. I'm sure he didn't mean any harm. I'll call in on Tuesday and pick up some washing. I've written it in your diary so you'll know. Bye, bye."

At tea-time that day, Albert did come again. Hilda was in the kitchen, preparing her tray, when he called to her, bold as brass, from the lounge: "I'll take a brew if the kettle's going on. Splash of milk. Don't be light on the sugar."

Hilda couldn't believe it. How had he got in again? She fumbled for her walking frame. Slowly, she scrubbed along the tiles to the lounge, careful not to push too far ahead. He was on the sofa, reading his paper. The cheeky so-and-so had taken off his boots!

Before she could speak, the microwave pinged.

"Tha dinner's ready," he said, rustling the paper. "Don't s'pose I'll be getting that cuppa now."

Hilda jostled the walker back towards the kitchen, trapped momentarily between two rooms. She paused to take a breath. It was a long while coming. "I shall have to eat my dinner standing up, thanks to you."

Albert turned a page. "You don't want to be doing that."

Hilda didn't, it was true, but what choice did she have? It was a struggle to eat in the lounge nowadays. The cod mornay would be cold by the time she'd put it out, wheeled the trolley to her chair and got herself settled. It was the same with yesterday's corned beef hash. A skin on the gravy. Dried peas. Cold mash. She tugged at the walker. Stupid thing, if it wasn't snagging on the carpet it was sticking to the tiles.

"You want some oil on those wheels," said Albert. "You don't want to be toppling over, you know."

Of course she knew. Another fall and Stephen would talk about a home again. Hilda didn't want to be in a home. This was her home, even if the stairs were an effort and those boys were always leaving things around to trip her up.

"Nowt on the telly again, I see."

Albert was doing the crossword now. Hilda gave an exhausted sigh. She didn't bother with the telly any more. Three sets of glasses and she still couldn't work the silly remote. And Stephen got annoyed if she rang to ask.

"Buzz off," she said, taking Rosemary's advice.

Albert put away his pen. "Where to?" he replied.

Hilda bobbed her head, unsure of what to say. She hadn't expected a question from him.

He asked another: "If tha could go anywhere in the world, where would it be?"

Hilda leaned into the walker. It was uncomfortable, standing up for this long. It made her arms ache. And if her legs went stiff she would have to press the button. Pressing the button was hard with one hand. It might mean another fall.

She turned her head towards the patio windows. "I should like to sit out on the Green," she replied.

On one of the benches that faced the sea. Kind people walked their dogs on the Green. If she waited long enough, the dogs would come to her and she could stroke them and feed them a biscuit each. She had some in the under-sink cupboard, she thought. Proper dog biscuits. The ones her precious little Monty had liked.

That was what started her towards the sink. She was certain she knew where the dog biscuits were: in a plastic box with a dark green lid, next to where Rosemary stored the bird food. With any luck those horrible boys hadn't found them.

She placed a hand on the worktop to steady herself. The walker tipped, but she had to let go of it to open the cupboard. There was the box, just like she'd remembered. A small rush of triumph filled her heart. She took the box out and shook it by her ear. It rattled like a biscuit box ought to rattle. But she wanted to see them, to count them if she could. Her gnarled old fingers reached for the lid. Blow these things. Why were they always so blinking... tight?

When she opened her eyes, she was on the kitchen floor. Daylight was filtering in through the blinds. A smell of cod mornay lingered in the air. She must have slept, she thought. She'd been here a long time.

"Blow me, these biscuits have seen better days."

Albert was standing over by the fridge, a dog biscuit lodged between his forefinger and thumb. He sniffed it twice, then tucked it away in his waistcoat pocket. Hilda couldn't see without turning her head, but she knew there were more biscuits scattered on the floor. The under-sink cupboard door was open.

"You're not one of *them*," she said. She meant the paramedics, the nice men and women in their crackly green overalls who came to pick her up when she'd had a fall. "I pressed the button *three* times, you know."

"Helps if you press the right side," Albert said.

Hilda groaned in defeat. She'd done that before, pressed the wrong side of the button. That was another thing that made Stephen angry. "Are you going to help me up?"

"Aye, if tha like." Albert reached out a hand. It seemed to stretch on forever.

"You have to lift me," said Hilda.

Albert shook his head. "Can't be doing that." He beckoned her up.

To her surprise, Hilda rose and took his hand. It felt comforting and warm, not at all rough. "The door's open," she said. And it was sunny outside, so bright she couldn't see the cars or the Crescent.

"There's a bench on the Green wi' your name on it," said Albert. "Shall we go and have a sit?"

"All right," said Hilda. "What about the mess?"

Albert closed the door on the mess. "I wouldn't worry about that," he said.

When you hang the family out to dry

by Kik Lodge

Shortlisted, Edinburgh Flash Fiction Award 2024

There's a north wind. You shake out the grandfather – who doesn't know he's your grandfather – and he growls. The washer has faded him, or maybe shame has. You imagine the motions of his lips twenty years prior, when he tells his pregnant daughter – your mother – to *give birth and give it up!*

You are 'it'.

The grandmother – who doesn't know she's your grandmother – has clumps of detergent in her hair. Her crumpled fingers try to swat you. *Bad egg*, she says, and you pin her cuffs to the twine with coiled fulcrums.

You peg the dripping aunt – who doesn't know she's your aunt – on the end. The same end in the photo you have, where two sisters stand in Peter Pan collars.

You only got given a month with your mother when you found her address. Questions turned to tears collected in a bowl. Her answers – *too young, too trapped, too stupid.* One month later, pathosis.

What are you going to come back as? you asked her.

The north wind.

Dare you, you said.

The family flap in front of you. Limbs twist and unravel, eyes sink, look away. Skin drips. Stiffens.

You think of the time you weren't with the grandparents in Yellow Cottage. When you didn't build a snowman with the cousins and get scolded for catching a cold. When your mother never hush-hushed you to sleep.

Do you know who I am? you ask, or maybe you bellow.

I cancelled the comics

by Jane Broughton

Shortlisted, Edinburgh Flash Fiction Award 2024

I thought of it as my cocoon and used to love lying in the gap between our settee and the wall. The triangular den was so narrow there was no space to turn around but I'd spend hours there. I'd rest my head on the velvety flocked wallpaper and marvel my way through a stash of Supergirl comics.

'There's only room for a tiddler like you, Mary,' da used to laugh. He'd peer over the top, round shiny face like a sun beaming down. His breath would be a minty breeze wheezing down the ravine and ruffling my hair. Sunday afternoons were our favourites when he'd lower down the latest weekly adventure, put his finger to his lips then settle down to watch his home team.

I knew if I kept quiet mam and da wouldn't always bother to check behind the settee and would talk freely. It was how I gathered my most useful information, morsels I could barter with Jade, my older sister. I'd warn her when mam was on the warpath. In payment I'd get sherbet lemons, chocolate bars and even, occasionally, silver coins.

But I was too slow the day da's breath stuttered from wheezing to gasping. I was shouting his name as I struggled backwards out of my sanctuary. I finally emerged in time to witness mam's panic and da's silence.

In the hours that followed I sat curled like an ammonite in a corner of the settee. Supergirl hadn't saved the day.

Lo Svedese

by Hollie Newton

Longlisted, Edinburgh Short Story Award 2024

He was there again.

It had snowed the night before. A 'shooting snow', that took farm workers from their beds to light torches amongst the vines, and hunters from their duvets early, in search of the fresh tracks of warm bodies looking for berries in the early morning light. And now the hunters were propping up the bar and testing her reserves of cherry wine and her patience with their bellowed *saluties* and worn tales of Mario Pepe, the fabled wild boar the size of a Fiat, 'eyes like the hottest place in hell,' and Lorenzo's brush with death in the frigid Pesa.

"Thought I'd lose my balls to the ice", he cries.

And they laugh. Roar. As though this was the first recounting. Hot breath filling the rough plastered walls with the aroma of fortified wine and rolled cigarettes, as lunchtime's rich peposo arrived on steam from the kitchen to tempt the belly and huff up the windows looking onto the snow-covered square. And it was hot. And it was suffocating. And it was too loud and too warm and too much and not enough.

Signora Baldi let out a breath she hadn't known she was holding. Heavy. And paused polishing what was possibly the cleanest glass in all of Chianti. The glassware of Enoteca Baldi was always spotless on mornings like these, her tea-towel used as a sort of armoured 'I'm extremely busy' shield to avoid getting drawn into conversation with the old bastards. Fifty-three years in this village. Amongst these men. Behind this bar. She placed the glass back on the shelf and turned towards the window.

They could have been anywhere. Three millimetres of condensation-clouded glass stood between her and the iced world behind. Quiet. Blue. Cast adrift on winter. Signora Baldi pulled the sleeve of her cardigan down over her hand and wiped a small circle in the pane. She could feel the cold through the wool, and for an irresistible moment felt like putting her cheek against the pane. To feel the ice against her skin.

She lent forward.

And saw him.

Across the road. Sitting patiently under the lecci tree.

Che palle. She'd be damned if she was going to have a customer freeze to death at one of her tables. There was nothing for it but to make her way to the door, pressing past the hulking uomini and their salacious remarks, while quietly cursing the man and the dog in the square and, yes, taking it as something of a personal insult actually. Why not come in to order, for god's sake? Hat. Coat. Signora Baldi flung open the front door of the enoteca and emerged onto the step where she made a great show of wrapping her scarf around her neck three times in a way that said, "Look. Look how I struggle," to her audience of two. With a final flourish she pulled her coat about her, to really underline the effort it had taken – the great favour she was doing – to serve the fool, and stepped onto the pavement into…

Silence.

Snow silence. From somewhere in the woods a jay called, a single cry that only served to draw attention to the otherwise blanket absence of sound.

It would snow again soon. She could feel it in the air. Clouds hung low and pregnant above the village at the top of the hill. A held breath. *Mio Dio.* There he was. The hardest winter in thirty years, and where does he sit? Outside. Same table, same chair, seven inches of snow around his ankles. Man and dog, for all the world a couple of tourists on a warm summers day. *L'Inglese.* The Englishman. He had arrived sometime in August. The height of silly season, when no one could move for bloody tourists and Hitler himself could have passed unnoticed amongst the bustle. But soon the crowds had thinned. And the days had passed. The weeks. Until it had dawned on the Signora that, every day at the same time, the same man would come and sit at the same table on the same chair beneath the same lecci tree.

It was a good position; set slightly back from the other customers, and sheltered from the sun by the shifting shade of oak leaves rather than her umbrellas. A Campari, always, for him. A bowl of water for his mangy dog, who insisted on occupying the chair next to him, sat right up at the table like a human – as though it was the most natural thing in the world, for goodness' sake. And from this vantage point they would simply sit, stringing out their five Euro order, watching life pass about them in the small piazza. The odd car passing by. Dario the butcher closing (early) for lunch. The Bianchi boys playing in the fountain.

A bitter wind found its way through a gap in Signora Baldi's scarf. The Englishman. He was a puzzle. And as anyone could tell you, Signora Baldi didn't trust things she couldn't understand. The Firenze Santa Maria Novella bus timetable? Unlike others, that was something she could get to the bottom of. But here was a mystery that no one could solve; a man who appeared every day, ordered the same thing, then quietly disappeared back to wherever it was he came from. She could see him quite clearly now. He was perhaps halfway through his life, and yet all of the seasons, all years, were visible in his face. Time seemed to move differently around him. As though his life had frozen at some point.

And he hadn't even been English to start with.

Lo Svedese. That's what she called him. Blue eyes. Blonde hair. Quiet and well mannered. Reserved, even. And tall. Swedish, clearly. And if he hadn't gone and visited the post office to renew his visa, handing Signora Brambilla a *British* passport, of all things, *Lo Svedese* he would have stayed. And yes, there may be an argument to say that it wasn't his fault he was English, but it had made Signora Baldi feel silly. And now of course it was one of the village's great jokes and would remain so until the day she died. And over time she had taken to simply arriving with their drinks, placing the dog's bowl right on the table.

"Grazie mille," he would say from beneath his battered hat, sitting and watching, lost somewhere between here and the past.

Signora's boots crunched in the snow. Creak.

"Hmmm. The same sound her as her knees," thought the dog, who very much looked forward to seeing this nice lady every day. She smelled of liver and beeswax floor polish and would hand him small scraps of prosciutto, or maybe a little salami, when no one was looking, her hand slightly open behind her as she set the drinks on the table. But today: something different. No drinks. The lady had forgotten.

The Englishman looked up and smiled. A question. For the first time in their near wordless six-month relationship, Signora Baldi had arrived at his table without their drinks. In fact it was only as she bent to serve them that she realised she wasn't holding anything in her hands. And in that same moment she realised that she'd been driven by a feeling so overwhelmingly hurtful that she had to almost physically swallow it back down. It was maternal. Something in her Italian conscience couldn't let her serve cold Campari and an iced bowl of water to these two fools on a minus two-degree morning in the snow.

She had little English, and the Englishman not much more Italian, but Signora Baldi had world class gesticulations. Would he like a bamaba, maybe? A bombardino? No? A cherry wine, then. Anything to warm the daft boy up.

"No grazie," he smiled, "uno Campari per favore. Grazie. Mille."

Signora Baldi threw her hands up in shrugged despair and turned. *Che idiota.* What more could one do? If he wanted to die from *il colpo d'aria,* so be it. The English were madder than any of them could have imagined.

"*Lo Svedese* wants an aperitivo," she announced to the bar as she returned, much to the merriment of the hunters.

"No herrings?" They laughed. "He'll lose his balls to the ice just like Lorenzo!"

"The two eunuchi of Panzano!"

Signora Baldi took down the bottle of brilliant red bitter liqueur, threw a handful of ice into a tumbler, and poured. Some soda. A slice of orange. She considered leaving the ice cubes from the dog's water, but would he miss them? A small dish of tarallini then, still slightly warm from the oven. And into her pocket, a few scraps of salami.

Outside, the first few flakes had begun to fall. The temperature had dropped, and the dog's nosed twitched. Charcuterie was approaching. He sat up, scruffy tail beginning to wag, as his dear friend appeared, the holiday clink of ice cubes announcing her arrival at their table.

Allora. Signora Baldi set down the tray and handed *L'Inglese* his drink.

Just as he reached out to take it, and quite accidentally, their hands touched. For just under a second, skin touched skin. And it should have been mortifying. Unbearably intimate. And yet. "É bello qui," the Englishman said, gesturing to the view before them. And somehow the moment had passed with ease. It was indeed beautiful. Still and white. Warm lights in every window in the village. A thin fragrant steam rising from the bakery set slightly up the hill from the square. Fountain frozen in time, water turned to icicles mid-fall. Funny how it takes a stranger to make you look at your own home properly. Signora Baldi chanced a look at the young man beside her. When was the last time that someone had touched her? Somehow, the barrier of communication between them had broken. She felt easy in his company. And so she stayed a while. The flakes falling harder now.

Until she remembered herself. She couldn't be hanging around here forever. She had a bar to run. And as if on queue, the sound of a glass smashing inside her enoteca broke the spell. *Quegli bastardi!* As she pulled open the door of the bar light and heat and raucous noise spilled out. In the fading light of the square, two figures sat beneath the lecci tree. A man. A dog. Two drinks.

Breakwater

by Gillian Webster

Shortlisted, Edinburgh Flash Fiction Award 2024

I slip into the water like a seal, sleek in my wetsuit, zipped and tucked. Spring's milky sunlight limns my arms with each forward stroke. Weightless, my mind empties. A pink float bobs behind me, an extracorporeal lung proving that I'm moving, still breathing.

We form lines, keep pace. I ignore the cold numbing my cheeks, the salt in my eyes. Breathe, legs kicking, arms soaring and slicing. Someone grunts and I smile, lips fused in a Vaseline-slicked grin.

Then, deep water and panic. A terrifying memory hunts me down, its black shape slithering below the surface. Quietly, I fight. Eyes closed, face down, I plow on; counting, clawing, and kicking to outrun its clammy grasp.

The leader yells, 'Turn!' and we flip. Fife to our right, Portobello on our left. Colourful houses shimmer above the broad expanse of sand. My arms begin to tire; I grit my teeth and kick harder.

Exhausted, gasping, I stumble up the beach. I am laughing as I wrap my Dryrobe around me, my magic cloak. Friends stagger over: sodden women and shivering men plucking t-shirts and jogging pants from a seaweed-festooned breakwater that's as vibrant as a weekday washing line. We share flasks of steaming coffee, form clots to chat, surfing the endorphin high, our ragged crew ready to face the week.

My mother drowned herself in our bathtub. I was ten years old. My brother taught me to swim.

'As if that will save you,' my father slurred.

How little he knew.

Miami

by Tommer Peterson

Shortlisted, Edinburgh Flash Fiction Award 2024

When I awoke
the house was on fire

> My first thought was to
> turn loose the chickens
> Maybe a free chicken dinner
> would distract
> the soldiers long enough
> for me to slip out

The small bag
I had so carefully packed
sat waiting for this day

> Gunshots and shouts
> covered my tracks
> to the secret beach

All I had to do was get past the reef
the current would carry me

> When the tide ran slack
> I turned into a dolphin
> and towed my small canoe
> until I reached the port city

From there
> The gold coins
> carefully sewn in the hem of my bag
> would buy me

a makeover
new clothes
shoes
lipstick

I would emerge
a stylish American lady
with sunglasses
a wedding ring
a stolen passport
a stolen credit card
and a gun
a first-class ticket
to my next chapter

The City
a long way from home
Loud and reeking of cars and sex

So many languages
So much money

My gold coins had since run out
But not my luck

I cleaned rich ladies houses
while they chirped to each other on colorful plastic
phones
about younger men and municipal bonds and magic
spells

The smell of roasting goat
led me to an old neighborhood

And then
thank the heavens

to a quiet brown poet

who spoke my language
and sang to me the meanings of my dreams

I baked a
Pan Patat
and washed the sheets

That was all it took

All the Time in the World

by Neil Gordon Shaw

Shortlisted, Write Mango Short Story Award 2024
Longlisted, Edinburgh Short Story Award 2024

With spooky timing, Roberto's text arrived just as I was opening my laptop to Facetime my husband...

Afternoon Charlotte. How about this weather – not the Glasgow I recognise! Gonna be glorious tonight too, so took liberty of asking for table on terrace. Hope that's ok! Looking forward to meeting you. See you soon! R

The superstitious part of me wondered whether the timing was some kind of sign. Certainly it didn't do anything to assuage the stupid, low-level guilt I was feeling about our date tonight.

I messaged back a thumbs up and, for the zillionth time since we'd connected last week, opened the dating app on my phone and accessed Roberto Barone's profile.

I was, despite myself, still a little thrilled we had matched. On the face of it, Roberto Barone was highly fanciable – strikingly good looking in a rugged, Mediterranean way; consultant radiologist; and sporty – mountain biker, footballer, skier. Not the kind of guy I expected to find on a dating site, frankly. Maybe he was too good to be true. Then again, I was on a dating site and, even at the business end of my thirties, still highly fanciable. Maybe Dr Barone thought I was too good to be true.

So, it was obvious – I should definitely go on the date, definitely not back out.

And what was the worst that could happen? A stilted evening at the trendiest restaurant in Glasgow, with a very handsome guy who I'd never need to see again.

And if it went well?... In his profile picture the good doctor was wearing a t-shirt that showed off his broad shoulders and muscular arms, and for a moment I allowed myself to daydream about being in bed with him, being in those arms, being ardently consumed by him. And I felt that urge that these days never seemed to be far from the surface – an urge now tempting me to jump in the shower and get creative with the shower wand. But I wasn't going to succumb. Not right now.

Right now I was going to speak to my husband.

'Hello, Lewis Gemmell, you gorgeous man!' I said, when he appeared on the screen. That rush of excitement whenever I saw Lewis never seemed to fade. He was sitting at the table in our kitchen, behind him the blurry background of the bay window that faced out to the Campsie Fells, a few miles north of Glasgow. He looked as good as he always did – today in a pink work-shirt I hadn't seen before, the colour just seeming to quietly emphasise his masculinity.

'Well, this is a lovely surprise, Charlie. Wasn't expecting you till later.'

No-one apart from Lewis ever called me Charlie. I loved his names for me... When he was being tender, "Torrie" – the name my younger sister called me before she could say "Charlotte"; "Dobber" when he was exasperated with me; "Miss Appleworth" – after the minor private school for girls I'd attended – when he considered I was being prissy or naïve. What was that saying about the loved child having many nicknames?

'Where are you right now?'

Where was I? The first place that came into my head –

'Dubai… I'm in Dubai. At the hotel.'

'Oh Christ, you have my sincerest, most heartfelt sympathies. How is Dubai these days?'

My sincerest, most heartfelt sympathies.

Maybe I was over analysing it, but those words didn't sound quite right coming out of Lewis's mouth.

'Dubai is as vulgar as ever.'

He was frowning and gazing at his screen.

'I'm looking at the weather there… Fifty-one degrees? You're melting, aren't you, you must be?'

'They do have air-conditioning, you know. I'm still very much in one piece.'

'I'll need to check that thoroughly when you get back. How long do I have to wait?'

'Till next week, Tuesday. Listen, I can't talk for long. I'm having dinner with… Olga, the new girl from Marketing.'

What a cow I felt, lying to him about tonight – absurd though it was to feel like that.

'But I'm missing you, Lewis. And we might not get the chance to speak later. So tell me, how was yesterday?'

'Oh, yesterday was superb. We did that hill, Stob Ban, means "white peak" – loads of white quartz near the top. Great walk, fabulous ridges, the cliffs just far enough away from the paths, thank you very much. And the day was entirely midge-less, although Hammy was right about the clegs. What a pain in the arse they are – actually *literally*, on two occasions yesterday. The first time it was Hammy's arse, then mine, the latter event being, objectively speaking, significantly less amusing than the former.

'Twats the lot of them, the clegs. That'll teach us to wear shorts.'

This was the Lewis I loved – hearing him speaking, in his very Lewis manner, about the mundane details of his day – that's what I treasured most about chatting with him.

Had I always felt like that?

We talked, in the effortless way we had, about nothing – what he was having for his tea, that MP who'd resigned for fiddling her expenses, work. And when we stumbled onto the subject of Paris we got to reminiscing about the holiday we'd had there in summer 2030.

'Remember that old dude who had the apartment opposite?' said Lewis. 'The one who only ever dressed in purple?'

'Oh God!' I laughed. 'I'd forgotten about Monsieur Mauve!' I was continually impressed by Lewis's powers of recall. I supposed I should have been used to it by this time.

I'd lifted my eyes from the screen for a moment, and was gazing out through the kitchen's bay window, thinking vaguely how lush and inviting the Campsie Fells looked this afternoon, and telling myself that I was cutting it fine, that I'd need to get ready for Roberto; and Lewis was in full flow, extolling the charms of the old café beneath that Parisian apartment. And then it happened...

An unambiguous bum note.

The first unambiguous bum note in weeks.

'... those splendidly delicate little pastries...'

Splendidly delicate little pastries. Lewis would never have uttered such a phrase. Not like that, not without irony, not in a million years. Of that I was certain.

Then he was saying, 'Look, I know you've got to head, Charlie, but Hammy and Sara have got an apartment in Verona next year – for the whole of June, the bastards. There's the option to join them for a week. We don't need to decide now. Verona is fantastically situated, by the way...'

As Lewis enthused about Verona, I was thinking about the message I'd send Everlasting regarding the bum note. They would, I knew from past experience, do the necessary finetuning immediately – it was part of their eye-wateringly expensive aftercare scheme, which I'd been sure to buy as an add-on to their criminally expensive standard package.

Everlasting... arguably the one silver lining adorning the big black cloud that constituted living in the most surveilled society in the world – a UK company leading the way in the A.I. reconstruction of dead people's personalities – drawing on every website the subject had ever visited, every social media comment they'd ever made or liked, every phone and Facetime call, every text message, every personal email. And, if you supplied Everlasting with such things – which I had done – videos the subject had appeared in, digitised versions of their old diaries and of old cards they'd sent. Up to whatever date you chose – in this case 15 December 2036, when Lewis's stage four melanoma was discovered and our world imploded.

None of my friends knew I had Everlasting. They were all telling me that, after eighteen months, the clock was ticking and it was time to move on. And they were right. Despite its name, despite the convincing illusion it provided, Everlasting no more bestowed immortality on a person than a photograph did. Dead was dead was dead. Perhaps now was the time to put an end to it. I wouldn't even need to have the conversation with Lewis – I *couldn't* have the conversation with Lewis, for goodness sake, for the obvious reason that Lewis no longer existed – I was, at the end of the day, just engaging with binary. I could pull the plug right now, simply uninstall Everlasting, and the only being that would feel the slightest thing would be me. And the main thing I would feel would be – surely, finally – closure.

And then I noticed the Lewis on the screen studying me, that wry smile on his face and twinkle in his eye, an expression I recognised so well.

'Torrie?' he said gently, mischievously.

'Yes?'

He placed his hand on his screen and before I could stop myself, I was mirroring the gesture.

'You're perfect, you know that?'

'Thank you, Lewis.'

I could feel myself welling up.

'I think it's only responsible to let you know that, from time to time. You are perfect and I am so, so lucky to be your husband.'

Tears were streaming down my face. This was just what he could be like, exactly what he could be like, and this feeling... this was exactly how special he could make me feel.

'And, I have to say, even with your nose flowing freely like that, even with the mucus and the snot and whatnot, you look so indescribably beautiful when you're crying.'

'Thank you.' I was laughing through the tears, dabbing at my eyes and nose with a tissue.

How could I turn my back on this, how could I just throw this away, sever this precious, precious connection to the man I still loved more than anything? And how could I contemplate breaking the spell by getting involved with someone else – 'moving on', when that was the last thing I felt like doing?

I picked up my phone.

'Lewis, I'm going to text Olga and make my excuses. It was just a loose arrangement for dinner tonight, really – I'm not hungry right now anyway – and I'm so enjoying talking to you.

Perhaps we can speak a little longer? I'd like to talk more about Paris, maybe?'

'Of course, we can, Torrie. We can talk for as long as you like. We have all the time in the world.'

A Winter to End All Winters

by Faith Cobaine

Shortlisted, Edinburgh Flash Fiction Award 2024

The house overlooks the bay. A window is open, lets sea air in. The hall, painted burgundy, almost visceral, is crammed with framed photos – babies, graduations, weddings, her late husband.

She sits in the kitchen, fills the void with radio phone-ins, shuffles of a newspaper, tea, poured from a pot, clinks of cup against saucer. Little routines.

They'll be back soon, spreading mess and life. Coats and boots and bags, bragging and boasting of promotions and plans for next year. They'll bring needless gifts, drink too much, eat late, leave pans in the sink, cans on the table, footprints on the stairs.

Mornings will be silent, warm, delicious; they'll rouse just before noon; rare lie-ins, respites from the race of their working worlds.

Like teens again, they'll yell from the top landing, splash bathwater onto the floor, spray choking, scented sprays.

The ancient feather-filled sofa will be flattened by their weight, and they'll find renewed novelty in the binoculars on the sill; a moment taken to glimpse ships vanish beyond the horizon.

She'll try on their energy, like a jacket that no longer fits, and find a long-ago smile, abandoned, bittersweet, in one of the pockets.

Board games. Cards. TV. Laughter.

On the first Sunday in January, they'll hug her, say they'll see her at Easter, and she will nod, play along, knowing they will not.

When they're gone, she will close the windows, cancel the papers, the milk, and decide how and when her winter will end.

The Alchemy of Mints

by Sue Dewey

Shortlisted, Edinburgh Flash Fiction Award 2024

Extra Strong

My father was not the kind of man to hold hands. He held a finely sharpened chisel and a pitted metal mallet to drive it into stone. He could loose unicorns from their chains, summon majestic lions to roar, and soothe their cuts with tissues of gold. His workshop sparkled with dust from language excavated from Blue Slate, Granite, and York Stone; from words turned inside out. Heraldry and lettering were his art. Cathedrals and embassies his canvas. 'Royalty keeps me in work and you, princess, in coloured crayons' he'd say, this man of toil and sweat, of skill and sensitivity. So, when I watched the car boot dip with the weight of his carving, I fancied it curtsied to a Master.

He never carved memorials. 'I don't like sentimentality' he said. And yet whenever I tugged at his pocket his hand would emerge, fingers unrolling foil as precious as platinum, unveiling something as desirable as a kiss.

Best Before

Years later I found this packet in his jacket pocket straddling a hole. So here I sit with his emptiness draped over my thighs like a pound-shop Pieta, squinting at a darning needle. As I sew, I imagine myself the artist, painting the Sistine Chapel's ceiling, animating my would-be-again man. There! With this tug the gap closes.

'Best before October 2014' the wrapper states, the year he died. Now, as I return this packet of mints to his pocket, I can finally feel his hand in mine.

Poor Creatures

by Miriam Needham

Longlisted, Edinburgh Short Story Award 2024

Two women stand close together on main street in Ballybofey. They curl in towards each other, almost meeting at the nose. From far away they look like an arched doorway: solid, pointed. They speak in low voices now, in almost-whisper.

'Isn't it awful.'

'Yeah-yeah-yeah.'

'Isn't it awful what she did to him.'

'Yeah-yeah-yeah.'

The woman on the left, Maggie, sucks air in through her mouth every time she says the word 'yeah'. Her head nods along in rhythm with the conversation. She nods and agrees even during the gaps when nothing is said.

'Yeah-yeah-yeah.'

The other woman, Carmel, wears a serious expression, her eyebrows set in a straight line. Every time she says the word 'awful' her eyes bulge slightly, as though they are trying to leave her head.

'Awful, awful. Poor Kevin. Awful!'

Up closer, they look less like a doorway and more like a barrier. The air between them is full, dense. When Carmel speaks next, a piece of spittle flies from her mouth and lands on Maggie's coat. Neither of them notice.

'Awful what she did to him, and him only doing his best, all this time.'

'Yeah-yeah-yeah.'

They have just bumped into each other outside McElhinney's. Maggie is on her way out, having just bought clothes for her grandson (socks with trains on them, a t-shirt with a train on it, pyjamas covered in trains). Carmel is on her way in, on a mission to find shoes that are comfortable and also suitable for a christening. Now they stand paused. They are a few metres to the left of the automatic doors, directly in front of a large window display. Behind them, the mannequins on the other side of the glass are wearing last season's trends, now at 20% off. Maggie's left arm hangs straight, shopping bag dangling from her fingers. Her right arm is tucked into itself, thumb hooked around the straps of her handbag. Both of Carmel's hands are curled around her handbag straps, pulling down on her left shoulder. She pulls the handbag down harder now for emphasis.

'Him trying his best with her and then she goes and does this. Up in the middle of the night like that. For God's sake. Up and out like that. Out of nowhere!'

'Yeah-yeah-yeah.'

'No consideration for the child at all. Only thinking of herself. Selfish. *Selfish.*'

'Yeah-yeah-yeah.'

'Poor Kevin.'

'Yeah-yeah-yeah.'

Carmel re-adjusts her handbag to stop it slipping off her shoulder. Maggie slows her head-nodding to stillness. They both look downward now, their gazes landing somewhere on the footpath, their minds travelling on parallel roads.

Inside each of their chests a feeling grows: something like love, or pity, or need.

Above them, clouds are passing, unrushed, vague. There is hardly anyone else around. It is mid-morning on a Tuesday, in the nowhere-space between school runs and lunch breaks. A gust of wind carries a crisp packet down the footpath. Across the street a gang of pigeons bicker around a bin. A tractor comes barrelling down main street, and then Carmel tilts her chin up. There is a steadiness in her eyes now, a doggedness.

'He did everything he could. Everything he did was for her and the wain. And then to turn around and do this to him.'

Maggie's face has crumpled in on itself and hardened. Her lips have all but disappeared. She says it sharply:

'Yeah-yeah-yeah.'

Behind them in the window of McElhinneys, the mannequins wearing last season's trends serve as an unwitting audience to Carmel and Maggie's conversation. There are three mannequins on display: a tall man-mannequin with broad shoulders and a blank face wearing a suit; a thin woman-mannequin with a long neck and no head wearing a blue shirt dress; and a small child-mannequin in yellow dungarees. They are earless, impassive, plastic. They listen to the conversation happening in front of them as best they can, which is to say, they do not listen at all.

'Mental health, apparently. But to be so cruel. So *callous*.'

'Yeah-yeah-yeah.'

'All of a sudden, up and out like that out of nowhere!'

'Yeah-yeah-yeah.'

'And getting the guards involved and all! I mean talk about *drama*.'

Maggie stops nodding her head, looks at Carmel now, whose eyes reach even further out of their sockets, darting this way and that, before landing back on Maggie again.

'You didn't hear?'

Maggie shakes her head once and then goes completely still. Behind her, the headless woman-mannequin waits patiently and calmly to hear what Carmel has to say. The tall man-mannequin remains steadfast and upright, a column of certainty. The child-mannequin between them stays quiet, pretends not to listen, but listens all the same. Carmel's voice comes in a fast pulse now as she runs over the details.

'Well she called the guards in – into the house, into their home – called them and told them she needed *help* – made up some kinda thing, d'you know – said apparently that she wanted them there for safety – safety? – safety? – can you believe that? – and the poor wain was petrified of course, didn't know what was goin' on, all of a sudden these two big men in uniform at the front door, and sure Kevin didn't know what to do – poor Kevin – it was such a shock for him – all this drama out of nowhere – and then off they went and the guards wouldn't even let him follow them – wouldn't even let him follow his own *son* – and he didn't get to see the wain for two weeks – *two weeks*, would you believe – poor lad – sure all he did was look after them and she goes and does this – makes all this *drama* over nothing – mental health apparently – mental health my eye – but sure you never know what's going on in someone's head really do you? – you never know, you just *never* know – someone might look normal but they're just hiding it all underneath – and she was always up and down apparently, always up and down – poor Kevin – him doing his best all this time, just trying to be a good husband and a good father and putting their needs above his own and then she goes and does this – does *this* – the *guards* and all – drama – *drama* – for what? – *for what*? – isn't it awful, awful, just *awful*.'

Carmel pauses to catch her breath. Maggie's mouth is a large O, and her eyes are two large Os as well. The information hovers in the air between them. Maggie breathes it all in, into her wide-open mouth. Behind them the mannequins react as blandly as ever. Above them clouds are moving, diffusing light. Across the street two pigeons tear at a crisp packet. The tractor is still heard in the distance.

Maggie lets out a long, audible exhale and shakes her head slowly. Carmel tightens her grip on her handbag straps.

'And now poor Kevin havin' to ask for permission just to see his own son.'

Maggie flicks her tongue off the roof of her mouth and makes a sharp tutting noise.

Clouds part and a slash of sunshine falls along the street. The entire storefront is suddenly bathed in light. Carmel squints unbeknownst to herself.

'Can you believe that, can you? Havin' to ask for permission just to see your own wain.'

Maggie sucks air in through her teeth.

Behind them a retail assistant enters the window display, sidling through a small gap at the side. He makes his way over to the headless woman-mannequin, hunkers down and starts to unscrew her from the stand. If the woman-mannequin had a head and could look down, she would see a bald patch surrounded by ginger hovering about her feet. The retail assistant stands up, puts his hands on her torso to keep her steady. He is sweating a little bit. He stands behind the mannequin and hugs it around the middle, tugs upwards.

'And the *lies* she's told just to get her way. I mean getting the guards involved, for god's sake. Pretending to be some kind of a *victim*.'

'Yeah-yeah-yeah.'

Behind them, the retail assitant tugs harder. The headless woman-mannequin is proving difficult to remove. He strains, readjusts his grip and yanks harder.

'Anyone who's ever met him knows he's a gentle soul, knows he wouldn't hurt a fly!'

POP! Off she comes. The retail assistant stumbles backwards with the effort, putting one arm out to regain his balance, holding the mannequin around the middle with the other. He steadies himself, wipes his brow. CLACK! One of her legs falls off.

'Him just trying his hardest to manage, and her with all her *moods* and all her *drama*.'

'Yeah-yeah-yeah.'

He leans over to pick up her fallen leg but as he does so – CLUNK! – the other leg falls off too. Flustered, he loses his grip entirely. She clatters to the ground, plastic limbs bouncing and clacking. His mouth makes the shape of 'for fuck's sake'.

'The lies, the lies, just to get her way. Selfish. Anyone who knows him knows he wouldn't hurt a fly. Some day and age this is when you can just say anything you want and be believed, pretend someone's done something bad to you and then you can do whatever you want, twenty years ago there'd have been no daddy, she'd have had to give up the wain or go to England, but here she's had everyone taking care of her, looking out for her – after all the *ruckus* she's caused – and now she goes and does *this*?'

The retail worker bundles up all the body parts and sidles back out through the narrow gap into the shop floor, knocking the stump of her neck off the wall as he leaves. In another moment he is back inside the window display, unhooking the man-mannequin with ease and sidling back out through the gap again.

'Isn't it awful.'

'Yeah-yeah-yeah.'

'Isn't it awful what she did to him.'

'Yeah-yeah-yeah.'

Behind Maggie and Carmel, the child in the yellow dungarees waits alone, a blank face of expectation.

'That child'd be better off without her altogether.'

'Yeah-yeah-yeah.'

A drop of rain falls on Maggie's nose, making her blink. They both look up. The clouds have joined together again, stitching up the seam of sunlight that had fallen through. Another drop of rain falls, this time on Carmel's forehead, and runs down her cheek. She pulls her coat around her and lifts her shoulders up towards her ears. Maggie brings her shopping bag in front of her, grabbing the plastic tight to keep the new clothes dry. They both look up at the sky, now a blanket of grey, not even a peep of sunlight getting through.

Carmel puts her hand on top of Maggie's, gives it a little squeeze.

'Don't get soaked. Be talking to you.'

Maggie squeezes her hand back, nods vigorously.

'Yeah-yeah-yeah.'

They part, Carmel scurrying into the shop, Maggie heel-toeing it quickly to the carpark.

Rain is pouring steadily over Ballybofey now. In no time at all, a trickle of rain has become a downpour. The street has emptied; even the pigeons have run for cover. Puddles are forming in the dips and curves of the footpath and water drums noisily on every surface. The sound is immense: like a million tiny darts being thrown over and over.

Behind the glass, the child in the yellow dungarees is quiet, quiet as a mouse.

A Temporary Dilemma

by Charles Maciejewski

Shortlisted, Edinburgh Flash Fiction Award 2024

I got in quite a tizzy.

I opened my shopping bag expecting to see a fresh head of cabbage, but what I found instead was the head of an elderly gentleman.

I'd been on the bus with my best friend Aggie. We have the same type of shopping bag. She's married to a brute of a man, a bully and a philanderer.

I'd been telling Aggie to get rid of him for forty years.

Now here he was looking up at me, although his complexion was far less florid than I recalled.

I was in a quandary. What to do, what to do?

Fluffy is a very fussy rabbit, and I had no cabbage left in the house.

Fortunately the doorbell went, and there was Aggie holding up my bag and looking rather sheepish.

'Wrong bag' she said, smiling.

'No harm done' I said, 'Fancy a cuppa?'

Fluffy enjoyed her fresh cabbage whilst we had a laugh about the mix up.

Aggie has put a red ribbon on her bag so we don't confuse them again.

Russian Bookshop, London, 1991

by Kathryn Aldrige-Morris

Shortlisted, Edinburgh Flash Fiction Award 2024

Gorka lets me into the shop, switches the CLOSED sign to OPEN, and does his thing where he goes to say something but doesn't. I want to ask *What?* But I can't. Maybe it's the being late again. He flicks his lighter and goes out back to smoke *Celtas*, the ripped-out filters scattered below the cashing up desk. I watch him tap ash into a rusty samovar and open his *El País*. He's a good boss. I unpack *Pravdas* tied like hay bales with red string, stamped with Cyrillic postcodes, slotting them into the newspaper carousel, rotating it to pull out the old news.

Gorka joins me at the cash register. Now there's the both of us waiting in silence for the door to open. He coughs, then says he likes my pussycat moustache. For a moment, we freeze. We look at each other – the possibilities compressed within that look: him leaving his wife, his mouth on mine, a life in the Basque country! But a customer brings what feels like the Siberian wind into the shop and Gorka retreats for another smoke.

In a few months the Soviet Union will collapse. Gorka will flip the sign CLOSED for good and we'll box up the books and sign on the dole. A year later, I'll hear Gorka died of lung cancer and, like everything else that decade, I'll wonder from behind another empty bookstore window how it is we see the signs of what's coming, but still. The shock.

Worm Your Way Out of This

by Roger Meachem

Shortlisted, Write Mango Short Story Award 2024
Longlisted, Edinburgh Short Story Award 2024

Sunshine pours into my plush apartment as I brush the leather top hat. This hat doesn't match the early 1800s bishop's garb I've hired, but if questioned, I'll say it's been bought during my travels.

Nearby, an Edinburgh tram clatters past as I compose myself comfortably on the sofa, folding a single page from a newspaper into my pocket, having checked that it bears today's date, 24th February 2023. The rough obsidian gem that I keep on a simple silver chain around my neck I hold firmly in my fist, and I place a finger on a favourite page of *Pride & Prejudice*, then read aloud, 'Good gracious! Lord bless me. Only think, dear me. Mr Darcy. Who would have thought it?'

As I softly speak further from the Austen novel, a familiar sensation courses through me.

Those few, those very few of us able to slide avatar-like into authors' imagined worlds describe it variously – often poetically: Drops of mercury slipping between fingers, releasing a trapped moth from cupped hands. My grandmother, who gifted me the obsidian, told me she heard angelic voices when she wormed her way into people's creations – she wrote historical novels set in Russia. Me? I simply feel my toes curling. It takes all sorts.

'What detail!' Her reviewers would remark. 'How deeply she has researched the period!' Hah! All Gran ever did was read a few lines of Chekhov, Turgenev or Tolstoy, and she'd be inside a nineteenth-century Russian country estate. A few hours later, she'd return, her writer's notebook brimming with detail.

I've no wish to be a writer. Writers can starve to death. In any case, I'm too lazy to set finger to word processor, so I've become what some people call a thief. But just ask yourself, is re-positioning particular objects from one world to another theft? Really?

Right now, toes curling, I'm preparing to visit the home of Austen's fearsome Lady Catherine. Dressed in the guise of a missionary bishop of the time I'll say that I'm seeking alms for the newly established Missionary Society's Calcutta School. Once in her mansion, I'm confident I'll be able to liberate a few Regency crowns or other portable silverware. Modern Edinburgh is costly for someone with my tastes. Lady Catherine de Bourgh will be a challenge, but the man who's been able to cadge a whisky from Rick Blaine and steal a kiss from Sike's Nancy knows no limits.

She's not at home! A problem with descending uninvited into someone else's imaginary world is that it isn't your world. You don't control it; you can't skip to your favourite bit. Austen's characters live their own lives outside the pages.

In the absence of their gorgon-mistress, the staff welcome the young, informal Bishop who brings them sweetmeats from the Indies (Turkish delight from my local convenience store). It's Lent, and I'm asked if I'm fasting. I tell them, 'I'll pray and fast on my voyage back to Calcutta. If I fast now, I warrant there'll be no bishop remaining by the time I land; my flock wouldn't see me if I turned sideways.' Within five minutes, I'm being plied with cold partridge and small beer. In return, I regale them with a suitably gripping adventure supposedly set in tiger country.

'Lord Bishop, sir, you'll frighten everyone.' The housekeeper speaks sternly enough but smiles while the housemaids and manservant sit entranced.

I continue, 'Most humbly, I threw myself onto the mercy of the Almighty. Tigers behind me, fierce warriors to both sides. I clambered higher and higher. The pressing danger giving me fortitude. My hands were cut, and my knees bruised. As I reached the clifftop, I shouted the Lord's praise.'

I'm confident I could make my living as a storyteller if I weren't doing so well with literature.

As I finish my meal, I see a plate of water crackers being taken upstairs and learn that Lady de Bourgh's curate is inhabiting an upstairs library, preparing his Lent sermon.

Being full of food and beer – a devilish notion enters my head – to tease Austen's comical Mr William Collins.

I'm led to the library but dismiss the maid before pulling myself to my six-foot height and flinging the door open.

'Mister Collins, I believe. William Collins.' I use a commanding tone.

'My Lord Bishop.' He jumps up, dropping a tome and knocking an ornament to the floor. As I stand and watch, he scrabbles to collect pieces of pottery. I can hear him mutter, 'Oh, my lady. Oh, my noble lady, forgive me.'

I stride forward to interrupt the poor wretch. 'Don't concern yourself with trifles, Collins; I'm here to meet the man Lady de Bourgh has written to me about, the man whose moral character she speaks of so highly.' I hand him the card I've prepared for this visit. It introduces me as Bishop Timmons of Calcutta, residing at Windhover House, Coates Crescent, Edinburgh. This is my address in the 21st

Century. In Austen's time, that entire street had yet to be built.

The man is jittery and bends to pick up his book. I take it from him firmly.

'Cruden's Concordance. Quite a read you've set yourself.'

'Oh, my Lord, my Bishop... my Lord Bishop, I find it aids my thought. It gives me... gives me...'

'Gives me a headache even looking at it.' I set it down on the nearest table alongside a pile of handwritten notes, the Sunday sermon, I'm guessing. A plan has come to mind. There are none so temptable as those who preach against temptation. 'Your hands, sir, why they're blue. You're cold. There's no fire in this room! A mulled wine, at least.' I pull on the bell rope.

I demand that he drinks the wine, and Collins, clearly no drinker, begins to let down his guard. In case Lady Catherine returns, I test the curate's knowledge about Calcutta. He shows no interest apart from remarking that he's heard the place can be hot. I regret now having done so much homework on the subject and change direction.

'So, this is your sermon, William. Eight, nine, ten pages, I count. Ah! Corinthians, First Epistle and a favourite passage of mine.' I refill his glass. 'You work too hard, sir.' He attempts to retrieve the pages, but I ignore his fumbling. 'It's a common fault amongst dedicated clergymen like yourself. It leads to a dulling of the edge of your wit. Come, I've something to show you,' and stride out carrying his notes, leaving him no choice but to follow.

I lead the way to the games room. It was the talk of the kitchen, something the de Bourgh woman had installed at no little expense to lure her nephew Darcy back to visit her. Hasn't been touched, I was told.

Collins starts back on entering the room. I'm confident he hasn't seen this or any other Carom-Billiards table. He splutters.

'My Lord!'

I'm uncertain whether I'm the addressee.

The man is just as susceptible as I imagined. I've almost had to command the poor devil to take up a cue, but after teaching him a few basics, we're away. Poor fish. He's never imagined that there could be such amusement. Despite some of the misshapen balls – I think Lady C. has skimped and bought unseasoned ivory – he's so taken with it that he accepts a whisky from my flask. His Lent accreditation is well gone. He forgets to keep an eye on the sheaf of sermon notes, and it's no problem for me to extract a page and pocket it.

I leave him in ecstasy, sending for more drink and cue tips. There's no sign of his patroness, but in any case, I need to get back. Even if she doesn't find him hard at play, there'll be ructions tomorrow when he tries to deliver an unrehearsed, incomplete sermon while hungover.

I find a Rococo-style mirror in a guest bedroom. It's a little unwieldy to carry but should be worth the trouble. With my pockets full of silver (the locks on these Georgian strongboxes are easy pickings for a man trained by Raffles), I find a deserted room, read out the date from my newspaper, hold the obsidian, feel my toes curl, and I'm home.

Outside, the sky is dark and lightly-clad youth streams along the tree-lined street towards the watering holes. *Pride and Prejudice* lies discarded on the sofa. Tomorrow, I'll take the mirror to a useful acquaintance. There's a hefty commission, but it'll save me having to explain yet another valuable antique to some strait-laced auctioneer.

I lie back on the sofa and debate whether to return to Austenland and visit Pemberley or perhaps try a bit of Chaucer country. There's huge opportunity for acquiring antiques in those Canterbury Tales. A buzzer sounds. It's the concierge.

'Gentleman here for you, Mr Timmons.

'Too much trouble to ask for a name, Mungo?'

'Bit strange looking, Sir.'

'Two heads? Snake eyes? Oh, never mind!' You could die of old age before getting sense out of Mungo. 'Send him up.'

I'm still in my Regency bishop's outfit, but anyone rich enough to live in these apartments can wear what they like. I open the door with a flourish.

The man standing outside is top to bottom in late Victorian middle-class costume. Derby hat, frock coat, waistcoat, trousers and scuffed boots – all faded black. He looks to me like some Dickensian detective.

'Bleak House's Mr Bucket, I presume?' I ask him while smirking at the joke.

'Shuffle at your service.'

There's something in both his tone and look that straightens my face.

'You must 'company me to a place where you will be 'eld pending a 'vestigation into several thefts.'

I've often expected a visit from the police, but this? This is laughable. Confidence surges back.

'Theft? I''ve stolen nothing in reality. You'll have a hard job proving...'

He interrupts me. 'I'm with JARB. Justice for Authors 'gainst Rogue Bookworms. We 'ave reason to believe you are such a one.' He places one beefy hand on my chest and, before I can react, reads from a book he holds in the other. 'The end of an unclouded day. Almost a happy one. Just one of the 3,653 days of his sentence, from bell to bell. The extra three were for leap years.'

Too late I recognise the final line of Solzhenitsyn's *One Day in the Life of Ivan Denisovich*. Shuffle's hand grips my obsidian gem, and I feel my toes curl.

I find myself next to what looks like a prison fence; wooden huts behind me, a vast frozen waste in front. I struggle to hold myself upright against the freezing wind of the Gulag Archipelago. Shuffle, at my side, puts his mouth to my ear.

'You'll be 'ere while we decide what to do. Can't 'ave the likes of you bothering characters. That Mr Collins was found drunk on top of a billiard table. Ee's in a world of trouble with Lady Whosit! You can't treat people that way, Mister Timmons. You need to think about what you've been doing. We don't mind bookworms, but you're a rogue, a bad un. You 'ave a good ponder while you're 'ere.'

'How did you find me?'

'Left your calling card, didn't you? 'Ad your proper address on it. Just 'ad to find when Windhover House was built and scouted through the years 'til I found you in it.'

I realise that he's taken my gem from its neck chain. 'You can't leave me here dressed like this? I don't speak Russian! I can't live on cabbage soup, Shuffle. Shuffle?'

But he's gone, and without my stone I'm stranded.

There's a tap on my shoulder; a gruff voice says something I can't understand, but I guess I'm being asked: 'Who the hell have we got here dressed like a dummy?'

Banned from the supermarket

by Susan Osborne

Shortlisted, Edinburgh Flash Fiction Award 2024

Dear Mr. Cornthwaite,

I'm asking you to reconstitute banning me from your supermarket. It was an over-reaction to a set of circumferences beyond my control.

I tied Rocky up outside, so was surprised when he escaped. Kevin Grimshaw untied him on purpose. I have had alterations with him, in the past.

Rocky has never been inside a supermarket. He loves sausages, and being a big dog, had no trouble reaching the butcher's display.

I could have got him to walk out quietly if the butcher hadn't chased him. Rocky's feet couldn't grip on the tiled floor, so he skidded. If he hadn't been perused by the butcher, he wouldn't have colluded with the fruit tower. I'm not to blame for the apples rolling everywhere. There has been a miscartridge of justice.

The screaming lady shouldn't have pushed her trolley at Rocky. He jumped over it, but the butcher didn't and ended up riding it into the washing powder display. That's why he was on the floor, covered in washing powder with apples and shopping all over the place.

All that pandora was an unfortunate sequin of events. Rocky ate the sausages, so I can't return them but I will pay for them.

I feel it's unfair that I am blamed for the instants.

Now you have the full story, I hope you will feel dispersed to reconstruct your decision, as I have my eye on the sunbed offer which starts this Sunday.

Best regards,

Edith May Pinkerton

Cry of the Kittiwake

by Mary D'Arcy

Longlisted, Edinburgh Short Story Award 2024

I stood on the seashore that damp Sunday afternoon, hair tangled by the wind, phone buzzing in my fist, my thoughts so balanced between dread and hope as to fix me in an attitude of pained immobility.

Kittiwake, Cathy-wake.

Above my head a seabird squawked, iterating its own name. Or so it seemed to my fraught and humming nerves. In another age I might have taken that sharp nasal cry as a warning to rouse myself and tread with care.

Answer him. Take his call.

I looked at the phone, but didn't pick up.

Back home, I filled the kettle at the sink and made myself tea. On the window ledge the cat stared into the courtyard, her knife-blade pupils following the movements of a crow but not allowing it to disturb her peace of mind. She yawned, drew a circle round herself with her tail and settled down to peaceful sleep.

Sleep, innocent sleep... balm of hurt minds.

I sighed, set down my cup, and as I shut the window against the distant cry of the gulls, a sudden weight of loneliness and desolation struck at me, crushing me down. So that when, later in the evening, the phone rang again, I didn't hesitate to answer.

'Hi,' I said. 'Sorry I missed your call.'

I surprised myself by managing somehow to master my emotions. Yet I couldn't help the faintest tremble in my voice. We talked desultorily for several minutes then, yes, I said, when without warning he turned the conversation. Yes, I'd received his mail of the week before. And no, I hadn't known that he'd fetched up in the States. And yes, I agreed, we could meet in town. Might I suggest a bookstore café?

I gave its name and precise location. And then I gave the day and time.

'Saturday,' I said. 'How about noon?' Adding quickly lest he ask me to forward a photo: `Look out for someone wearing blue.`

That much I owed him, I mused, as with trembling hands I ended the call. But after the first flush of doing the right thing was over and cool reflection resumed its sway, doubts assailed me.

Did I want to see him?

Would it put me in turmoil?

How, after all this time, would I seem in his eyes?

What would we talk about – his life or mine? All that had happened since last we'd been together? And what were he to probe? To delve? And having plumbed the depths, as it were, view me in a different light?

But... I drew a shaky breath... was he the type to delve? To turn over stones?

Doubling my hands, I walked up and down the narrow confines of my kitchen, pausing at the window to gaze out at nothing. It was a cool June evening and the shadows on the lane were lengthening. Soon it would be dark and I would be alone as ever in the stillness and no –

Never, never. It wasn't in him to probe.

To patronise.

His cello voice if anything had been flatteringly deferential, working hard to tamp down subtexts as he asked conversationally how life had been treating me (you have a job, did you say?), whether or not I were living alone (haven't married, have you?) and assuming I was happy (can you really be, without me?).

I had hedged a little which he took as the sign that he'd overstepped the bounds. He let a moment pass, then clearing his throat, struck out again. And I knew from the words he chose and the manner of their delivery that he was constructing a chart of my personality, carefully mapping the landmines, so he could travel without fear across dangerous terrain.

Almost did I smile. For I was listening more to his voice than to what he was saying. He touched on a variety of themes – his work, the recent past, a trip to Hawaii, his single state – rounding off with: `So then, Catherine, Saturday you say? I look forward to seeing you.`

We said our goodbyes, and a click put an ocean between us.

A week of anxiety would loom during which I was destined to pass from one mood to the next – from hope to grief to joy to remorse and swiftly back to hope again. I yearned yet dreaded to see him. I couldn't eat. My sleep was interrupted by frequent jolt-like awakenings.

Kittiwake, Cathy-wake.

To think of him rising up like that out of the swamp of the past. The shock of hearing his voice. And why, why had he left it till now to smoke me out when Time with its pickaxe was doing its worst? Look at me – thinning hair and thickening waist, hollows at temples and cheeks, lines running down from my nostrils, and on my brow – seared like a deep-grooved stigma – the furrow of my permanent frown.

But... I tried to reason myself into tranquillity... what is the worst possible thing that can happen? The worst possible outcome? He knows your age and what to expect. Are you really so boneless, so timid, so vain as to not want to let him see you?

Courage, Cathy, I enjoined myself. Ignore that voice in your head, lean into your fears, and go there.

Saturday found me clad in blue and casing the bookstore several minutes ahead of time. With a rattling heart, I climbed the stairs to the first floor, a gym-sized room with the layout of a public library. I had chosen it because it was as familiar to me as my bedsit, and because the Costa café which was tucked to the left commanded a view of the stairs.

But to my consternation every table was occupied. Abruptly, I rounded on myself. Why had I not foreseen this – Saturday, summer, tourists, family outings? And, oh, dear Lord, what if he's already here watching from the shadows, taking note of me before deciding whether or not to come forward?

Kittiwake, Cathy-wake.

Taut with tension, I looked across to where shoppers were browsing among the aisles and tried to force my stiff features into a semblance of composure. Turning back, something caught my eye. To the rear of the café two young women were rising together and scraping back their chairs. I waited till they moved away before sidling past them and claiming their table. Then, with a businesslike air, I removed my coat, slung it over the back of my chair and he was five minutes late. Rummaging in my bag, I found my comb and furtively ran it across my hair. When I looked up, I saw him.

Standing at the top of the stairs, gripping a bouquet of roses, and looking my way.

My heart gave one great bounding leap.

James. My James. Sauntering towards me, a smile on his face.

James. My James. Carrying about him some of the unmistakable majesty of his profession.

James. My James – a barrister.

My eyes glistened. And the consciousness that he had wanted to see me, had taken pains to find me, and had stopped to buy me flowers, was like healing balm on all the bruises of my battered soul. I tried to smile, but couldn't. Then slowly, against all my efforts, my throat tightened and my vision blurred with moisture. All I had planned to be – cool, indifferent, aloof – was now beyond me. But as I was pushing back my chair, getting ready to greet him, something curious happened.

He came to a stop two tables before me. Craning my neck, I saw the reason why: her jacket was a dazzling shade of blue. Burberry – just like the doctor, the woman I do for.

'Hi,' He held out the roses. 'Catherine, I take it?'

It was the voice I'd heard on the phone.

'I'm James.'

I sank down paralysed, wrung with dismay. Was this, then, what he'd expected, an elegant middle-aged lady, pearls in her ear lobes, bounce in her hair, smiling with a faintly amused contraction of her brow before telling him, No, sorry, she wasn't Catherine?

He inspected her, a little doubtfully, before mumbling an apology. By which time I was arming into my coat, head lowered with sudden blinding pain. I waited till he slewed the other way. Then, face averted, I scrambled past him and quickly down the stairs.

I no longer wished to meet my son.

Tea Leaf

by Jo Spencely

Longlisted, Edinburgh Flash Fiction Award 2024

I won't be welcome. Not after the conniptions over the teacups. How was I to know they're Royal Doulton?

'Take them,' Reenie had said, 'to remember me by.' Heard it as clear as if she'd spoken aloud. By then speech wasn't her strong point, but I could still *tell*.

It's the sugar bowl I'm back for. With those little tongy things. Not that I used them. 'You'd do the same,' I'd say to Reenie as I pinched a cube between thumb and forefinger, 'if you were still drinking tea.'

I sneak into the wake. Dry-eyed mourners clunk into each other like lawn bowls. Funny how people come flocking when a dead body's calling, isn't it? When they couldn't hear a live one?

Like Reenie's daughter there. Came twice a year and left behind an emptier house with every visit. I swerve to the refreshments table.

In a snap the sugar bowl's in my bag, the tongs tumbling after it. I'm reaching for the milk jug (not strictly part of the set, but ever so pretty) when the vicar's hand, more skeleton than limb, seizes it.

I freeze. I can't let him connect 'tea set – tea leaf – thief'.

'Curdled,' I hiss. 'I'll get fresh.'

To any man with a higher calling (God, money, learning), any woman is 'the help' so he hands the jug over.

The kitchen's empty. I pour the milk away, then escape down the side return, the china clinking its tiny applause at me taking what's rightfully mine.

Mopping

by Hannah Retallick

Longlisted, Edinburgh Flash Fiction Award 2024

between Mr Jonson's bed and the bathroom he'd tried to reach, staggering naked, trailing dysentery

down the corridor, throwing warnings to space-suited staff and pushing the bucket back with her heel, soap flicking like stormy sea foam

into the free cubicles, whispering you-okay under the door to a weeping young nurse, who's working a pandemic tsunami away from Spain

dodging next-of-kins surging past, their breath stifled by masks and fear, hidden tears cupped at their chins

internally, as she sinks into her car seat and grips the steering wheel, pausing to clear her mind before returning to

the mess she shouldn't have to clean up but always does because, because, because

in their kitchen, along the red tiles, swishing into the crevices while Jobless sits at the table, head rested on fists, exhausted from nothing

more vigorously now, into the utility room, where he can't see her but can hear her if he wants

in her mind, again and again, running through Mr Jonson's trailing dysentery sea-foaming corridor cubicles weeping homesickness you okay you okay you okays stifled tear-cupped next-of-kins drive home to the mess she shouldn't

have to clean up but does because because because
permanently furloughed Jobless who can hear her if he
wants but

through tears, feelings swirling, swish swish swish

the whole of today's story from the COVID floor.

Worms

by Elizabeth Hibbs

Longlisted, Edinburgh Short Story Award 2024

It started by accident, a roll of the dice, a fluke of variation. The rubbish was really getting out of control by then, 290 million tons thrown away each year in America alone, and every other country racing to catch up. The consumption was incredible and recycling was a joke. Of course, there were efforts to reduce. Calls to rationalise, protests and international conferences, self-help books, listicles: ten top tips for a simpler life. But nothing made any difference, until the worms.

It was 2027, before you were born, when they were first discovered. Quietly going about their business in a 300-hectare landfill in California, just eating trash. No one had noticed them before. They looked just like any other worms, to the untrained eye. Then along came that post-grad environmental science student, specialising in the rate of decay of compostable clingfilm at varying depths in landfill stratification. No one believed her of course, at first. It was too ridiculous. But in the course of her research she took some of those worms back to the Stanford University labs for independent testing, and as we now know, was proved to be correct: the worms were eating our rubbish, their novel, super-fast digestive abilities breaking apart the carbon bonds and long-chain polymers to transform Styrofoam, polyester, cardboard packaging, discarded plastics and e-waste back into the elements they'd been made from. It was only a matter of weeks before the media got hold of it. *Miracle of our times*. A solution to all of our profligate consumerism, our incessant hunger for things, our wasteful habits – a last-minute environmental reprieve. *Hope for humanity! Worms to the rescue!*

Before long the worms were big business. The fashion industry bought containerloads from the research labs in a concentrated greenwashing effort, sending regular shipments to help rehabilitate dumpsites in East Africa, where decades of their unsold stock and exported second-hand clothing had formed impermeable layers of synthetic fabrics in the ruined soil. In Kampala, Dar es Salaam and Nairobi, the worms were set to work, eating their way steadily through discarded nylon sportswear, polyester suiting and 'ocean plastic' puffer jackets.

Dairy conglomerates, in an effort to be seen as philanthropists, set up their own worm farms in Vietnam and Malaysia, and bragged how they were part of the solution, supplying the worms that would start breaking down the mountains of plastic milk bottles dumped by unscrupulous recycling distributors from the UK, USA and Australasia. The brand managers and marketing teams went all out making it sound like a massive, philanthropical expense, but really it was so cheap, and so easy. They multiplied fast, those early worms, and they were hardy. Low maintenance. Darkness, sun, cold; extreme heat, waterlogged soil or arid dust, they thrived in all conditions. All they needed was our rubbish, our recycling – and now we really could call it recycling. The true age of circularity had begun.

After that first flush of capitalist exploitation, governments took over worm regulation. The worms were seeded in every public landfill site in the EU and Australasia, as part of a coordinated inter-governmental effort to manage environmental degradation. In wealthier suburbs they were soon in every household wheelie bin, cultivated like pets, and in the slums and industrial estates they lived free-range, spreading from skips and rubbish heaps to colonise the gutters and drains of every town, in every country.

Quickly, the focus shifted off waste minimisation. No one was talking about overconsumption anymore, and the corporates breathed a sigh of relief – business as usual. Everyone could go back to splurging on fast fashion and shoes, doing up their houses, upgrading their phones on a whim. And those who could afford it did, with a renewed vigour. It really was a golden age for consumerism, an explosion of human creativity: whatever elaborate product you could think up, whatever pressing need you thought you had, you could almost guarantee that someone, somewhere in the world had manufactured it already, and if not, you could get it custom 3D printed and shipped to your door within days. Heaven!

But it didn't last. In our delight at having got away with it all, we'd underestimated the worms. They were hungrier than anyone expected.

Some said it was deliberate, guerrilla anti-growth groups throwing worm-bombs into factory windows at night, roaming the cities by day and planting worms in shopping malls and big-box electronics stores, sneaking them into data centres. Others said it was just natural evolution, a burgeoning worm population seeking new habitat, finding fresh food sources. But whatever the truth, the worms kept multiplying, and popping up in unexpected places, and as they multiplied we began to realise: they made no distinction between what we threw away and what we wanted to keep. Seems obvious enough, in hindsight.

The first I heard of it was here at our local museum. Someone had trekked the worms in on their shoes, maybe just one worm, who knows. It doesn't take much. Staff started noticing damage to paintings, and display cabinets. Then the electrics started to malfunction: worms in the wiring. The whole place was shut down for a deep clean, but it was too late. We didn't know then how easily they could spread.

Within days, it seemed, reports were coming through from overseas: government offices evacuated in Madrid, cargo ships stranded in the Panama Canal, Amazon warehouse quarantined in New Jersey. Our local bookshop shut down after a shipment of contaminated stock from the Philippines, and after that the public library closed, desperately trying to preserve their collection. Websites began to glitch and freeze as servers crashed. Communications were disrupted worldwide, and that made it hard to know whether we had it worse here or not. Probably it was the same all over. But while we were arguing about our clean, green status and trying to tell ourselves we were a country of safe refuge, the streetlamps started falling from their poles, one by one, and giant sinkholes opened up where the worms were devouring the infrastructure beneath the roads. And where were all the people we expected to do something about it? Good question.

It must be hard for you to imagine now how much we used to depend on them, the planners and decision makers, the politicians and providers. But remember, this was a time when so much was done for us, without us even noticing. Water in the taps, and electricity that came on just like that, when you flipped a switch. We never gave it a second thought. But when everything we were used to started to crumble, the people who were supposed to be in charge of it all were nowhere to be seen. Some barricaded themselves in their glass and steel mansions, cramming in years of supplies and hoping for the best. Others escaped the cities to their rural properties and holiday beaches, taking the worms with them as they went. I know, it's hard to understand what they were thinking. But try to imagine. You might have done the same, in their shoes.

The supermarkets here stayed open as long as they could, naturally, gouging a profit. The food was mostly okay, of course, but the way it was packaged made it impossible to keep on the shelves. Flour and pasta spilling out of degrading packets, Tetrapaks of milk and juice leaking everywhere. There were always lights flickering, a freezer defrosting, damaged patches of lino on the floor. No matter how much money there was behind those big retail chains, they just couldn't keep it all together. By then we were having to clean our shoes every time we entered a building, walking over decontamination vents in the doorways. Those who could afford to installed them in their own homes, but most of us just wore those disposable shoe covers, the blue elastic ones. You still see them around sometimes, caught up in a high tree branch, woven into a bird's nest, stuck in the window of a building high up, flapping away. They were just everywhere for a while, like a uniform. If you saw someone wearing them you knew they were at least trying, they were safe to be around, not one of those crazies in denial who might put your family at risk. I used to cross the road to avoid anyone not wearing footwear protection, for sure, even if I knew them. Well, that's what it was like. Besides, you didn't want to be in the middle of it all if a crowd got nasty, and turned on someone.

By then the borders were closed and trade between countries had all but stopped. Turned out some places' worms were more aggressive than others, and there was a desperate attempt to limit the spread of different sub-species in case of further mutations. People kept on moving around anyway of course, running from place to place however they could, but the flow of goods just cut right off. There were terrible shortages of all sorts of things we'd taken for granted, and we couldn't replace anything that the worms had damaged. We just had to make do with what we had.

It was easier for the rich, of course. They could afford to have their food delivered, packaged clean in glass or aluminium. For a while, anyway. They hoarded it, together with clean water, and solar panels, and their precious artefacts, and all the tech and gadgets they needed to keep them safe. A lot of them holed up in the tower blocks, fitted out with sophisticated decontamination systems and airlock doors. Money doesn't mean much now, but back then, it bought you everything you needed, and the luxury of control.

As usual, it was the poor who suffered most. At ground level only steel and stone survived, and all our old comforts were gone, food for the worms. The foams and fabrics that made up our homes, the thermoplastics and polyvinyls that our lights and heating depended on, gone. All the old ways of telling our stories, with paint, and print, and film. The archives of music, and history, preserved over the centuries. All lost. There was a lot of grief, at first, and anger. But we adapted, shifting into the shells of old commercial buildings, forming neighbourhood alliances and agreements over resources. Fighting neighbourhood wars. Eventually we settled into an awkward kind of peace, and now here we are, down on the ground, finding a balance with the worms.

We'd already started to grow our own food long before, of course, when the prices shot up. Tiny gardens in buckets and planter boxes, on little scraps of land round where we lived. But now we have the whole city, the vacant ground where the old wooden houses have collapsed, the rich aerated soil the worms have cultivated. No one goes hungry.

Your generation will never know the struggles we faced, or understand our nostalgia, not really. Those times are gone, but telling stories keeps the memories alive: the joy of renovating a weatherboard villa, the thrill of buying a pair of collectable trainers online. How it was to listen to a podcast or read a book, or make a phone call when something difficult needed doing, to get the people in charge to fix it.

In the old concrete and glass towers you can still see lights on here and there at night, figures moving behind the windows, far up on the top floors. They can't last much longer up there, guarding what they have, hermetically sealed in their worm-free homes. But we can't help them. Either they'll come down, or they won't. If you look up at the old Fujitsu Tower, up there in the corner window, you can see one now: a distant shape behind the glass. But who knows, you might be right. Your eyes are younger than mine. Could be it's just the shadows of the clouds, rolling and changing, a trick of the light.

We live in a town ruled by iron ore

by Cole Beauchamp

Longlisted, Edinburgh Flash Fiction Award 2024

Iron in the red soil we till. Iron running underground in veins of purple, yellow and gray. Iron that we drill, blast, tram, shovel in dark mine shafts and hoist into the light. Iron that stains our laundry yellow unless it's beaten and mangled in a vinegar solution.

We are well versed in disasters: air hose failures, frayed cables that crash the cages, cave-ins, water pump breakdowns, detonators that don't explode on time, crush injuries from chutes. Injuries so common the mining companies own a hospital. But not everything is covered when we are blinded, broken, killed. We embrace those left behind, consoling, cooking, cleaning, harvesting, repairing.

We wear our disasters lightly. After snow-blasted winters, we welcome the pleasures of blue skies, spotted fawns curling into their mothers. On Sundays after church we chat at the lake over picnic tables laden with Jello-O, frankfurters, potato chips, jugs of Kool-Aid. We swat flies and squash mosquitoes as laughter echoes over the water and children tumble, squabble, splash.

We are as malleable as iron, hammered thin when the shift boss says the rumours are true. The mines are shutting down. We do not break. We cling on until there's no more credit at the company store, no more free appointments at the hospital. Unemployment melts and reshapes us, anvilling some into new towns, chiselling others into mechanics and loggers. Those left behind inhabit a ghost town of weather-beaten mine shafts and deserted storefronts, sharing tales of how it used to be.

Apex Dilemma

by Candia Marsland

Longlisted, Edinburgh Flash Fiction Award 2024

Irresistible and fluffy with red satin bow the highlight at Christmas hugged close in the pushchair cheek to cheek every night tea-parties adventures escapades in the woods separation anxiety after first day of school guardian of the bedroom never abandoned treasured next to photos of Granny brilliant idea to import from Slovenia shy and retiring cute cookie faces soft rounded ears do you see how they scamper up and sleep in the trees rebalancing the eco-system in the alpine playgrounds of Europe sharing the bike-path 300 kilos live-cam magnet Italian tourism thriving exemplary mothers population exploded anthropisation stresses cross border to Switzerland 50 km/h top travel stealing the honey raiding the *pasticceria* mainly nocturnal consult encyclopaedia 90% vegetarian looking for nuts partial to corn appetite voracious small accident with the goats scarcity of berries wolves has Giacomo come home learning to live in *coesistenza* hiding the rubbish securing the door don't run away psychological flaw Spring is coming evicting white slumber nature's metabolism accelerates the church bells ring nearer a cow is missing outgrown their lair plantigrade feet towering height fear we think they are all tagged adorable cubs finger-long bone-colour claws carnival paws 42 teeth defensive assertive bi-polar disorder animal rights education threatened startled massive too close father son maul maternal instincts raw kill jogger *Spitzenprädator.*
 Spitzenprädator – apex predator
 Life Ursus – brown bear resettlement programme

The Tree Conservatory

by Sherry Cassells

Longlisted, Edinburgh Short Story Award 2024

They say the best time to plant a tree is twenty years ago. Same goes for telling the truth. Best time would have been right after Tom died – I mean what's another blow when the pain's already more than you can take.

We called my grandfather's acreage a *farm* at first although it was nothing like the neat green rows with scattered cows and bubble-gum pigs we expected. I couldn't get a grip on the size of the place though – acreage is difficult to quantify – it's like measuring peppers in pecks. When I asked him to explain my grandfather said *acreage is a state of mind.*

He called the farm a tree conservatory which was the main reason my father made fun of it, and when it was revealed to my brother Tommy there would be no *moo moo* here and no *oink oink* there, he didn't take it well.

Fuck's a tree conservatory? my driving father said, the stripes on his shirt fraying into the sky above our new convertible, my mother beneath a triangle of silk and perfume, her lipsticked mouth laughed, she turned to Tommy, *there there Tom, he's still got Minky,* but the old dog was no consolation and Tommy continued to mourn.

I thought the idea of a tree conservatory divine.

This morning I crash through the milestones going back.

It's been twenty years but change is gentle in the countryside, unlike the view from my condo where the skyline tumbles in perpetual flux allowing new buildings with strange shapes – there's one like a sail and when it overlaps the moon l feel an unmooring – but here on the road time has nowhere to display its progression save the trees, their differences also their similarities, and then into view hurtles the octopus oak I used to watch for, adorned with running shoes, each pair tied and flung over its boughs.

Tommy asked *why,* his curiosity rode him, filled him, and he demanded *why why why.*

I had an ability to count, was always and still am a counter, and it looked to me like an entire grade's worth of sneakers: 59 pairs, 118 singles.

My mother finally said *that's where somebody died, Tom.*

Tommy was easily reduced, as sensitive people go he was at the very quick, and the truth he pried out of our mother, that it must have been a young person who died, ruined him for the weekend.

Until that tree I don't think Tom knew that young people died.

Twenty years have turned the shoes grey, it's as if the tree is now bedraggled with Spanish moss, as if its branches have been hanged.

Next the tin house always catching the sun there's an increase in sooty blackness at its edges and it seems heavier, as if the hay fields wild around it are digesting it, the hollow farm houses further deteriorated, the three bridges also heavier, the locks at the Severn have been modernized, fishermen in boats bob here and there on the water while their black trucks wait on the shore like so many beetles, the cottages bordering the weedy lake have not been overtaken as my striped father predicted *poor suckers those joints'll be swallowed up in no time* and in Tommy's eyes I had seen it happen.

I am going back, crashing through, getting there. My window is open, the stripes on my shirt consider departure, I chain-smoke invisible cigarettes.

All along like clouds on the horizon the trees bubble, my quantifying mind goes on count again and I reel in the ever-accumulating sum. Tommy could count without counting too, but about the trees he'd say *there's only one you know, they are all together* and I'd look at him, catch his melting smile.

I remember how me and Tom hooted, exhilarated, when my grandfather showed us a sphere of dirt in the palm of his hand and said it contained more lifeforms than there were people on earth, the enormity of it thrilled us, the numbers in our heads jostled and spilled in a kind of euphoria.

I knew right away when Tom started using. I was not in his vicinity but I knew like roots know, I knew he was shooting up. I phoned him and said *what are you on* and he said *heroin mostly*. His confidence soared, his sensitivity was replaced with chunks of abandon, he yelled *it's like I am mainlining words I can talk to anybody* which certainly appeared to be the case for when I got home winded and alarmed there he was at the kitchen table talking to our father who sat silently in his pyjamas, flannel stripes dark and firm. The minute I walked in my father walked out like a revolving door.

Tom said *try some* and I did through my nose and right away we up and left barely fitting through the door we were many angled and splattered with inspiration we counted the stars and were up all night until shredded, we sifted through the door at dawn and to our beds, eerie and suspicious, for the doubts, absent for so many hours, returned uncountable, and I knew Tom's were exponentially heftier.

I have never been able to assemble my grandfather into a form, I cannot picture him, I know his hands were like my own. I remember the colour of his eyes. I'm told I walk like him – the problem is that in my mind he lives as a ghostly mosaic containing only the atmospheres of his conservatory – what eeks from dirt, the back and forth of oxygen and carbon dioxide, hurtling molecules, space, the fizz above Lake Superior over which pines loomed precariously, their upright brethren pulling for them he said, saving them, providing nourishment.

When we were young and subject to bedtime stories within the dark gnarled world of fairy tales I used to look over at Tom and take his hand under the blankets when necessary. My mother read the words as if she were dictating a distant weather report, our drunken father like Marlon Brando he bowed to the tale's Kings and fought its enemies, scorned the heroines for their weakness one night and their strength the next.

Our grandfather's house was smack in the forest where nothing is quiet ever, where slices of sunlight arrived scented with the breath of the whispering trees. I have tried to build his image from these visceral sections of light, too. It has become a sort of hobby. There are sparking moments in which he flashes like the hologram I saw at Burning Man, the summer Tommy died.

I always wonder the moment, for surely there was a beginning, when the terrain of Tom's mind began to distort, and then I have to wonder, in another realm of possibility harder to touch, was it ever smooth to begin with?

On my grandfather's land was a shoreline where the trees broke to allow rock. It was the edge of the Canadian Shield, the portion of continental crust underlying the majority of

North America, and there was something about its cool largeness I loved. I needed only count to one, and this rock dove into Lake Superior, another gigantic one.

The lake was named not because it's the better of the Great Lakes, but because of the French words for its position, *lac supérieur*, which simply means *upper lake*. The rock itself, the shield, eeks out pines along its edges – imposing beasts who dig their heels into scant earth – relentlessly shoved by the wind, their disfigurement is permanent and exquisite.

When I swam I felt I was up for digestion.

My grandfather remembered where each log used in the construction of his house had grown and he pointed over their billowing brethren in the forest saying to me and Tom, his disciples, *there's the beech, there's the ash, there's the balsam, the poplar, the maple, oak oak oak, hemlock, the birch.* Contrary to architectural norms and scientific laws he used all varieties of trees that grew in his forest, he felled them by hand, and positioned his logs vertically.

Nothing again will ever make me feel as safe as I felt within the walls of that house – my superfluous father, my simple mother, my savant grandfather, my brother Tom with whom I felt in a way conjoined, and my skinny young self whose job it was to protect everyone.

Within those walls I was off-duty.

When I think of heaven now it's not the usual paradise. It is the square interior of my grandfather's house plunked in the forest of my childhood.

Three hours jonesing for the forest.

I kiss my fingers fake-smoking.

Field rock cow field rock cow like Fred Flintstone running through his house table chair window table chair window field rock cow field rock cow.

When walking through a forest, look up my grandfather said and he continued to float words by us like objects – root-network, soil-fungi, light-dependency – we learned to trust our feet, especially Tommy who went ahead of me, his small feet flitting over the terrain swiftly and accurately while I stubbed and stumbled behind *look up, look up* my grandfather yelled at me while he marvelled at my brother's fluency. Tom's ears reddened with his praise, and the next day Tom tried barefoot, his white feet strange in the forest like ghosts.

Now I think the forest, in those fluid bare-footed moments, made Tom their own and he never again found peace anywhere else.

On the way home he hollered to stop the car and when my father finally pulled over we were right at the octopus oak and Tommy ran out, my parents started arguing, he pissed and then hurled his shoes up the tree and got away with it, his beautifully successful first act of defiance.

There is never a moment of truth, never a moment of revelation, there is only acceptance.

We went to the conservatory almost every weekend of our childhood. When I woke in the night Tom sometimes wasn't in the bed beside me, I looked into the square room's corners where he often curled but it was through the window I saw his feet like white rabbits among the trees. I lay back down, I can't tell you how frightened I was both *for* and *of* this moonlit stranger who came back to bed and found me crying, said *there there*, his cool hand reaching across the gap for mine.

It is a rare thing for me to lose count but by the time my grandfather died I'd lost count of Tommy's defiance's, our parents put the conservatory up for sale which alarmed me until Tommy told me it would never sell, that he'd had a word with the broker.

I have since purchased the acreage which is indeed a state of mind.

Tommy never tried to hide his drug use from me. He never tried to hide anything from me. We spent much of our time together even as our lives spread apart, and once a season, we went together to the forest, through the teeming landscape, beneath our father's faded stripes and the same pastel galaxies I drive beneath now, the road smaller smaller smaller closer closer here. My grandfather's house surrounded by his forest, his conservatory, where – had I told the truth – I would have put Tommy's ashes, not *scattered* them, but *put* them in the seams between earth and root, I would have pressed them into bark, packed them between needles, made a paste from them and painted leaves with their stucco, dappled some onto my own tongue.

Now for the truth: Tommy didn't die like I said. His body is not lost in Lake Superior. There was no heroic struggle unless his struggle with life itself was heroic. He died in the trees and I cut him down, planted him, and lied about it.

In the forest there are unwritten guidelines for etiquette.

A Whippet Arrives

by Susan Elsley

Longlisted, Edinburgh Flash Fiction Award 2024

Shelagh took the whippet home after she found it tied to a bench in the park. It sat on the rug and trembled, and she gave it a tin of beans because that was what was left. When she woke the next morning, the dog was lying next to her, a paw draped over her arm. A comfort after a month of slamming doors and a departure.

The dog came with her to work, and the others in the office aah-ed, making her feel like one of them again. That night she slept so deeply she called out when the dog licked her face at dawn. In the woods, it raced along the high path to the quarry cliff, and Shelagh jogged after it, scared that the dog might jump. Like she had wanted to last week and would have today, if the dog hadn't been there.

The dog didn't keep running when it reached the edge. Instead, it stared down at the moss-green water, as if surprised that the drop was there. It turned to glance at Shelagh, before disappearing up the path that led to the hill.

When Shelagh got to the cairn, the dog was waiting. She slid down beside it, reaching out her hand to stroke its golden hair. There was silence except for a skylark whirling above them. The dog leaned against her legs, its heat rubbing up against hers, and she swore never to walk the cliff path again, because nearly-twice was enough.

What do you think, Janey?

by Frances Dalton

Longlisted, Edinburgh Flash Fiction Award 2024

My dinner is at the Cape of Good Hope. I'm in Siberia, Daddy says, that's where I am. Lily in her high-chair is nowhere. Mam is in Alaska, closest to the kitchen. When Jam Jar comes to live with us he gets Greenland. He can't see the world on the oily cloth even though he wears big thick glasses. So Mam uses the clock instead.

"Meat at 12 o'clock, Dad," she shouts. "Veg at 3."

"Nothing wrong with my hearing," he mutters.

He makes as big a mess as Lily. She likes to grab her food and drop it in sludgy fistfuls on the floor. Jam Jar misses his mouth on the way up and the plate on the way down.

"Perfect," Daddy says under his breath, "Just perfect!"

Soft, after he's gone to bed, Mam says "Sure he's like another child."

She has to go to the bathroom with Jam Jar and aim his thingie at the bowl.

"You wouldn't do it for me," Daddy says.

"Don't be disgusting," Mam says.

They throw words about like it's a food fight.

"I'm telling you, your father's a danger to the children."

I think of leading Jam Jar around the house by the hand. He likes the feel of things, the smocking of my dress, the quicks on my fingernails.

"He's harmless," Mam says, "I should know."

"He wasn't always," Daddy says. "You know that too."

Then he turns to me and asks.

Blackout

by Rosalind Thomas

Longlisted, Edinburgh Flash Fiction Award 2024

My mother burned my books when I was twelve. She said they'd corrupt my mind. She said she burned my books because I was better off alone.

My mother made me watch as her fire began its wicked work. She struck match after match and their bright yellow arrows dropped noiselessly onto the books she'd spread open and their greedy tongues licked up the beautiful words until the pages roared back at me with angry orange mouths. My books bled their precious ink and I saw their spines buckle and warp like burnt meat clinging to brittle bones. I cursed my mother, wishing she too was burnt meat.

I gulped mouthfuls of book smoke, hoping to fill my lungs with those lost words, to draw their ideas deep inside me. Without my books, would I become more dead with every breath?

A plume of book-ash and word-soot whirled over my head, caught on a gust of wind. I pictured my books as a dark cloud of birds wheeling towards the coast. My love for my mother also burned that day.

She was scared of books, my mother. She feared they would steal me away from her, that I might choose the life they promised over the life she offered.

Words had taken my father away from her. My father was a writer. He left her pregnant because he needed words more than he needed her. Or wanted me.

I am a writer now.

Dark Horse

by Kate Wildersley

Longlisted, Edinburgh Short Story Award 2024

The first time you saw him was just after you'd been given the news, and you were lying amongst the fading grasses, watching the smoke massing dense and impenetrable over the hills – dusky-blue upon dusky-blue – the keepers were burning the heather again, scorching the Earth's skin to blackness, scarring the land with their fiery brands. Above you, on the hillside, the bracken and birches glowed like fire too – burnished copper, gold, yellow ochre. On the shore, the trunks of the pines blushed vermillion in the autumn sunshine, and only a few moments before, you'd been told there was a chance that you might live after all.

That morning, you'd walked along the moor road, breathing in the sweet earthiness of heather and bog, myrtle and moss, passing the graveyard where the ancient yews guarded the lichen-clad stones – it was there in the old kirk that you'd been married one summer's day, twenty long years ago – then you'd picked your way through the claggy field of barley stubble, startling a hare halfway across; it had run, panicking, away from you in long-limbed zig-zags; you'd always loved hares – gentle creatures – and following it out onto the ridge, you'd lost sight of it among the oaks.

To the loch you'd gone that hour, to be beside the softly folding waves, where the only other living thing to be seen, was the cormorant, perched on a branch of the waterlogged larch, drying his outspread wings. You'd gone there to seek solitude and solace – if you were going to be told there was no hope, where else would you have wanted to be but there? So down the bank you'd stepped, until you'd stood on the shore, rippling waves at your feet, light breeze on your skin, cold air in your lungs, and after a week of storms and gales that had raged like a tempest in your breast, you'd heard the words that breathed life back into you once more.

'Is there someone with you?' he'd asked, his voice a well of kindness.

'No, I'm alone.' Yes, you were alone, yet not alone – not anymore.

'Will you be alright?'

'Yes, I'll be fine,' Maybe you would be, maybe you wouldn't. Who could say?

'Are you sure?'

'Yes, I'm sure.' No, you weren't really sure. Of course, you weren't. How could you be? For all that you'd braced yourself in readiness for this moment, telling yourself that this was the end – prepare for the worst, accept your fate, and yet here he was, saying that, yes, it was bad news, terrible, in fact, but not quite as bad as you'd feared. You could be cured. You had a chance. All was not lost. There was hope. And afterwards, as you lay on the cooling earth, eyes fixed on the smoky sky, you wondered how you were going to tell your children.

Perhaps you fell asleep then – yes, perhaps that was it – as you lay among the fading grasses, and you only dreamt of the shadows creeping far across the loch, squalls tearing at the water, slicing the smooth ripples into jagged pewter slabs. It grew cold. You stood up – you were awake then – surely you didn't dream that. The wind charged towards you, ripping at your clothes, twisting your woollen scarf, tugging your hair. Your eyes smarted. Shivering, you pulled your coat close around you, and turned to go.

That was when you saw him. He was standing out in the loch, peaty water pouring from his head and flanks, forelock dripping, long mane trailing in the waves. He stood motionless, seemingly unafraid, and he was watching you. You gave a start – you hadn't heard or noticed him approach. Where had he come from so suddenly? Was his owner nearby? Someone was bound to be with him, and emerge from the pines to call him, then he'd wade through the shallows, dipping his great head in greeting, but, glancing around, you could see no-one else on the shore. You looked back at him, unsure of what to do – it was just you and a huge, black horse, as large as a carthorse, larger even. Would he charge? Was he friendly? You watched him warily and found yourself being observed with eyes, deep and fathomless, and into those eyes you gazed back, your breath caught in your chest. How long you stood there, either for seconds or minutes, you couldn't afterwards recall, but, by and by the horse lowered his gaze, turned away and, walking deeper into the loch, slipped silently beneath the waves.

You stood, staring at the spot where he had disappeared. Moments passed, but the horse did not reappear. 'Hey!' you shouted, 'Hey! Come back! Come out!' But there was no sign of him. 'Hey!' you shouted again. 'Hey – hey – hey,' your words came back across the loch, mockingly. You began to run, stumbling along the sand – perhaps he had come up near the pines, where the water was shallower, but no swirl of mane, or snort of nostrils stirred the surface there. You were all alone on the shore, and you'd just seen a horse, with your own eyes, walk into the loch, and vanish. For a fleeting moment you hesitated, then you turned and scrambled as fast as you could up the bank and out onto the ridge. The wind had eased; below you, the loch lay still, its surface a cloak of mirrors, a smear of silver, shimmering in a shadow-land of dreams.

As far back as you could remember, you'd heard tales of a kelpie – a water-horse – that lived in the loch. Your grandfather had told you of it when you were a small child, as you'd sat warming yourselves before the kitchen fire. He'd said that once, long ago, the kelpie had dragged three children beneath the water, and their drowned bodies were buried somewhere on the lochside, although you'd never found their graves on your walks alone amongst the bracken. It was just a dark tale from times past – not true, of course, simply a warning to children to keep away from deep water. But now you knew you were mistaken; your grandfather had been right – there really was a kelpie in the loch.

Or was there? Perhaps you'd only imagined it. Perhaps you'd dreamed of it as you lay on the shore, your mind a tumult of fear and relief, and you'd slid into easeful sleep, worn out by worry. Or was it the shock of the news that had caused you to hallucinate, to see a vision, an apparition, a *bodach*? And you lay awake each night, going over and over in your head what you had seen, and it had, it surely had, been real. Still, you told no-one about the kelpie, and for a long time, you didn't tell anyone about the cancer.

Three children you had, bright and beautiful. But now they were grown, not fully grown, not yet, but it wouldn't be long until they were, and their bright hair, that had shone like the sun, had faded over the years with their laughter.

Back through the barley stubble you walked that day, past the old kirk, along the moor road and up to the farmhouse, and no-one asked you what you'd been doing or where you'd been.

'When's dinner?' your oldest child asked.

'Where are my wellies?' your middle child said.

196

'Mum, can you wash these?' – that was your youngest, holding out an armful of clothes.

'How was school?' you asked, taking them from her.

'Boring,' she answered, without looking up.

Your husband sat bolt upright in his chair, staring straight ahead, a silence deeper than the loch between you.

As for the cancer, you left it as long as possible before you told your children, then as weeks turned into months, you struggled through surgery, scans and scars, whilst poison, distilled from the bark of yews, flowed darkly through your veins like a burn in spate.

Over time, sleep came to you again, and in your dreams you saw the kelpie, mane writhing like a voiceless nest of vipers, as it sank into the depths. Sometimes, in your sleep, you reached out to touch it, but your fingers became entwined in the snaking strands, and you were pulled down with it into the blackness. Over time, you began to doubt what had happened; you started to tell yourself that you couldn't really have seen a kelpie. They only existed in stories after all – they weren't real, and you breathed out long, slow breaths, and whispered, 'forget, forget.' Over time, you came to believe that you'd imagined the whole thing. The dreams faded. The memory dimmed. The cancer receded.

It wasn't until the following year that you went back to the loch. You walked there one summer's day with your children to cool down in water so dark from the peaty earth that when you stepped in to it, at first, it glowed amber and bronze like a fine malt whisky at your feet – wade in deeper, and it grew as black as in Irish stout.

Out into the loch, your oldest child swam. You swam alongside him for as long as you could but you'd never been a strong swimmer and you soon had to turn back.

'Don't go too far!' you called to him but he kept on. 'No further,' you shouted. 'Come back now!'

He did not heed you. On he swam, until, tiring at last, he turned around, but he was far out from the shore by then. Too far. You could see he was tiring, but he was still not close enough to touch his feet on the slimy pebbles that lay on the bottom of the loch.

'Come on, Finn! You can make it!' you shouted, but he was floundering, his arms flailing, head rolling – an eternity of effort to reach safety. Then, without warning, without making a sound, he was gone.

The water was ice cold – the summer sun was never able to warm it up – and you were out of your depth already, your clothes dragging you down. 'Finn! Finn!' You screamed, voice cracking in your panic. You grasped for him, searching, but your hands closed on nothingness. You could see nothing, feel nothing; there was just blackness – blackness and black, black water.

A shout came from one of your girls. You turned to see them both running into the shallows, hauling their brother onto the shore, where he lay, gulping for air.

'Something pushed me,' he gasped, when you reached him at last. 'Something pushed me to the shore!'

The grasses had begun to fade, and the keepers were burning the heather again, when once more, you walked along the moor road, pausing at the graveyard to break a switch from one of the yews that grew beside the wall. You twisted it with deft fingers into a circle of dark green needles, then you crossed the field of barley stubble – the hare was nowhere to be seen –and down to the loch, where you hung the wreath of yew on a branch of the waterlogged larch, where the cormorant had once sat, drying its outspread wings.

Then you stood at the water's edge, and you waited.

Kiss Me Sober

by Joan Murphy

Longlisted, Edinburgh Flash Fiction Award 2024

I want you to kiss me sober.

We sit in the shadow of a Georgian house. It makes us laugh to imagine the architect's reaction to the drunken women entangled on his front steps. "Is this what's become of my pride?" he'd ask. We pretend to apologise to him, we were too drunk to stand any longer. Our bus is coming soon.

I pull away from you because I can feel the question rising from my throat, to my mouth, to my lips, before I even know what it is. "Before I get my hopes up," I manage, "Is this you? or the drink?".

You shrink away from the question in a way that does not reveal your answer. I apologise because I want you to kiss me again. Is this what's become of my pride? I'm too drunk to remember that we've done this before, too love-stricken to care about the definition of

insanity.

In the morning you will wake up hungover from shame, and ignore my messages. I will stay up all night, waiting to crash violently down from the only high I have ever craved.

But right now, there are six minutes until the bus comes. I will spend three finding a place for myself in your arms, two tracing my finger along the creases below your smiling eyes, and my last praying that, next time, you will kiss me sober.

Kissin' Season

by Amy Macrae

Longlisted, Edinburgh Flash Fiction Award 2024

Soft yellow petals fall into the bowl. They dance on their way down as Jane deftly plucks buttery pieces of gold from in between sharp pines. She's laughing as she goes, not looking now, just feeling her way through her task as she throws her head back – a heady mix of heat and mirth flowing through her as her sisters dash around.

She loves the kitchen. Ma chopping, Grandma shilling and her sisters giddy and covered in school room chalk – all pink cheeked and wide-eyed. That smell. There's syrup in the air – the sweetness of summer that's simmering in a pot and the scent of the fresh wildflowers strewn across the table.

"It's kissin' season! That's for sure," her grandmother shouts over the chatter as the youngest children dart around the busy hearth.

"Ain't it always – that gorse grows wilder each year – stays longer too!" Jane replies, her eyes darting back to the cuttings – a playful smile teasing at her lips.

A touch. Jane thinks of him tracing the freckles across her cheeks. A circle of gorse guarded them from prying eyes as they basked in the rippling heat of June – just one golden hour before ma' needed her home.

"Are those petals ready or do I have to wait until Michaelmas, girl?" her ma' called over the din.

Jane passes the bowl over, catching the eye of her grandma as she did so.

"Seems everythin' in growing wilder by the day." Her Grandma says with a wink and laugh.

Mirror

by Ian Gouge

Shortlisted, Write Mango Short Story Award 2024
Longlisted, Edinburgh Short Story Award 2024

whose is this narrow face staring back accusation in the
eyes or regret or recognition or lack of any feeling and
squinting blurs its edges like wearing glasses with the
wrong prescription and when i do i see her reflected back
and it's uncanny this duplication being sprung from the
same mould more than a trace a physical form carrying the
imprint of history of legacy of betrayal telling the world not
everything about who you are although the world might
assume that but some part of where you came from her
history overlaid on yours like thin and crinkled carbon
paper you would consign to the bin as if in doing so the
past might go with it wipe the dna-slate clean allow you to
look in the mirror and say this is me not this is my mother's
daughter and when i was still a child i did childish things
played in the park invented games with my friends fantasy
was my motto and if we watched films to pass the time
movies nurtured that in me too perhaps one day or for
more than one day i was dorothy with my bright red shoes
toto the dog i could never have and how we skipped the
yellow road not cowardly nor made of tin or straw until in a
momentary glance perhaps a single frame smuggled inside
a scene the narrow face and in that face i saw and knew my
mother was the wicked witch come from the west's dusk
and into my life to taunt and torture me and she never left
she is here still not close but close enough not dead but
alive enough i can feel her malevolence as it travels the
motorways silently traverses the train tracks i can hear her

whispering accusations that nagging voice asserting my inadequacy and arm's length is not far enough nor is another city another county and sometimes when i am least expecting it i see her again the wicked witch of the west glaring out of the mirror and they ring me with updates the staff paid to care though how do you care for a witch and it's interesting how time has warped their tone the slide away from the upbeat away from encouragement the positive picture they were painting probably inaccurate unrealistic more impressionistic than anything as if i would fall for the soft colours the magic trick they were trying to pull verbal sleight of hand *come* they were saying *she wants to see you* they were saying standard patter bestowed on the absent all the while hoping to pass the baton for an hour or two to give them a chance for a chat put their feet up have a fag *after all we've earned it* and don't think i haven't noticed how over time the tone hardened the messages from the front-line less optimistic so i threw filters onto the phone and picked out their anger disappointment disapproval theirs as well as hers but i've done my time i want to say i'm a fully paid-up member even if i never wanted to be and i have the scars i see them every time i look in the mirror so why can't you *because you're never here* and perhaps more than fellow-feeling their desperation for relief trumped care triggered my panoply of excuses as i navigated further from the truth but they had their own filters too i'm sure of that *we've heard it all before* they never said but thought it and so in the end i gave them silence listened without hearing when they called and i took the phone to the bathroom and stared at myself as they spoke to remind me why i hadn't gone for weeks why i was silent why i didn't care and all the while i stared at me so she did too *i see the bitch every day* i wanted to say *i don't need to be there* i wanted to be snow white too and live that crude rural idyll so why shouldn't i have seen me in the mirror as a physical manifestation of

Disney's beauty raven-dark hair red lips beyond red
etcetera etcetera *mirror mirror on the wall* no prizes for
guessing who i did see and freud would have a field day the
only people i ever wanted to be fictional creations tied to
the black hearts of witches her soul probably needs
confession more than mine you know the rest so i chose to
move this far away a gap measured in hundreds not tens to
introduce impossibility so that i couldn't just hop on a bus
or jump on a train so that i could take myself out of the
equation cancelled out on both sides of the equals sign
lowest common denominator she would probably say *just
what i'd expect* and i absented myself so i didn't have to be
there to bear witness leave some poor third party paid to
disentangle her from her life's detritus the ornaments and
mementos photographs of other people souvenirs of other
lives anyone's but mine so handing the money over was
easy an antiseptic transaction my inverted version of judas
with no attendant unpleasantness absence and the heart's
fondness another myth so what would make a difference
what would transform my mirrored experience return the
bathroom cabinet to its right and proper purpose don't
think i haven't thought about it and her carers have hinted
at forgiveness though coy about where responsibility lay
who makes the first move and in their thinly veiled way
they have suggested she is ready but to speak or to listen
that's the question given a world of difference between the
two and there's an unspoken presumption that i might be
ready too to listen or speak and they suggest the recovery
of lost harmony is just one visit away as if there is a magic
wand to be waved to erase the years of demands and abuse
of victimisation and punishment of failing to live up to an
impossible standard or stoop down to it are slates ever
wiped clean i think not and in thinking not i disqualify their
premise so there is nothing she could say or i could hear
which would be salve enough *yes* i tell them *i will visit* but
only once more and on my terms when there is no need to

listen because she will be unable to speak and armed with black bags i will go through her things not with any desire to keep but to expunge for there is nothing she has in that putrid little oasis of hers her room in a bungalow of purgatory that i want nothing other than space the space vacated by her the silence from telephone calls not made and from requests i no longer need to deny and after that when i return home i will take down my bathroom cabinet smash its mirror put a new one up in its place

"Lovely day fir it"

by Hannah Ward

Longlisted, Edinburgh Flash Fiction Award 2024

And it is. There's nae need fir big brollies or warm coats. Folk ir in their gairdens, their skin soaking up the sun lit a greedy sponge. Weans ir in the park using jaikets fir goal posts. Neighbours ir hurling water balloons at one another wi reckless abandon. Dugs ir playing wi hoses and bairns wi sticky hauns ir splashing in paddling pools.

It's a lovely day fir it but ye wish it wisny. Why should the world keep turnin when yer own skited tae a halt? Why hisny the sky burst wi the weight of hauding yer grief tight in yer throat? Why hiv the heavens no opened? Is the sun taking delight in burning yer flesh as a yer heart is lowered inty the ground?

This dreich country, this grey village. Built purely tae escort wee boys fae the womb straight inty degrading manual labour fir mere buttons. This purgatory, where wee lassies ir chained tae their parents and then tae their husbands.

Hot tears obscure the vision of all attending. The one thing ye should be able tae count on ir the fat droplets spilling fae the clouds as they share yer anguish.

A thick smoke interrupts from a barbecue a block away. A stomach growls. A sad chuckle ripples through the gathering. The priest smiles.

Lovely day fir it.

The Man in the Park

by Eva Sneddon

Longlisted, Edinburgh Flash Fiction Award 2024

July 1964

You were flicking through a newspaper, occasionally looking up to check your boys hadn't tumbled off the swings or whizzing roundabouts, when you spotted her among the other children: a skinny girl squeezing two toddler boys into a battered pushchair. You leaned forward, your eyes absorbing her face, her smile, the way she pushed her hair behind her ears. Memories overwhelmed you.

You put out your hand as she trundled the pushchair past your bench. 'Wait, hen. Are you Nessie Kelly's lassie?' The married surname was bitter on your tongue.

Eyes wary, the girl nodded.

'I knew it! You're her image!' Except for the eye colour, blue instead of brown.

'Will you give her a message from me? Tell her Sammy Walsh is asking for her. Will you do that?'

A slight nod, a shy smile, then she continued shoving the rattly pushchair and its squashed passengers along the path. You watched until she was out of sight, hoping she wouldn't forget your name.

You never met the girl again, so you never knew that she did pass on your message, that she watched her mother's tired face soften and glow and wished it would keep that expression forever. And you never knew that forty-three years later, while clearing out her late mother's things, she found a studio photograph dated 1947, signed 'Love Sammy'. She recognised you, the man in the park, and wept... remembering the day your name brought a flush of happiness to her mother's cheeks.

Notes from Spring

by Lucy Donoghue

Longlisted, Edinburgh Flash Fiction Award 2024

Do you remember when you were a child, and you would drown petals in lime-coloured water, to suffocate their scent? *Jasmine*. The dregs of childhood bottled; the glorious concoction labelled 'perfume' in excited handwriting. Eau de Jardin.

She left on a Monday in May. *Lavender*. The final bouquet stood skeletal on the windowsill, putrefied and shrivelling. *Geranium*. Petals clung and then dropped down, down. I lost her when the water turned sour at the bottom of the vase. *Lemongrass*. Her scent is still tangible; earthy and impenetrable, like a garden in autumn. It's been a week.

White musk.
Sweet marjoram and fragonia.
Bergamot and magnolia and pine.

You could slice me open and pour her in and it wouldn't hurt at all. I would still absorb her like nectar. It's been a month.

I remember the first flower she gave me. A small daisy, meek and unassuming; it wasn't hers and it wasn't mine. It couldn't grow in my charity shop jug: it belonged to the ground, to greater things. And so, it drooped in a day.

The final flowers were sweet peas. They folded together like tissue, slow hands of pinks and purples grasping amongst the foliage, praying for salvation. But that never came.

She left on a Monday in May. Her base notes drip from the tap, sleep in the floorboards and watch from the walls. *Sandalwood*. Her middle notes are on my clothes. *Rose and neroli*. The top note is gone. *Forget-me-not*.

It's been a year.

Walk, Don't Walk

by Michael Callaghan

Longlisted, Edinburgh Flash Fiction Award 2024

It was a dark and stormy night.

I know. But it was.

The storm, as storms do, raged. Above a crossroads junction, a cloud, dark and deep and bloated, hovered and trembled. With a reverberating crack, lightning lashed from it, splitting the traffic lights below...

...flooding them with the fire of the gods....

Green Man blinked.

I am here...
I am me...
I...
...am...

A hand reached in front of him. He looked up, saw a familiar face.

Red Man.

He took the hand. And they ran.

They ran along the street, and kept running. They ran until the city opened up into fields and trees and moorlands. They ran, and felt the wind on them, the rain, the rising sun, felt the urge and surge of life gush through them. And as they ran, they hollered and laughed and shrieked.

Until, at the top of a hill, they stopped. The sun was now fading from their newly discovered world.

"We can do anything!" said Green Man. "Climb Everest! Swim with dolphins! Take a rocket to the moon!"

Red Man stayed silent.

"What?"

"It's just... I've always told people when not to walk," said Red Man. "You told people when to walk. We had... a purpose. People looked up to us. Literally. We... belonged"

Green Man thought. It was true. Anyway, he couldn't swim. And Everest was *very* cold.

He sighed.

"You're right. We'll go back. But... let's watch this sunset first."

And, hand in hand, that's what they did.

Scottish Arts Trust

The Scottish Art Trust was founded in 2014 and has established itself as an innovative and forward-looking charity that has a far-reaching impact on the arts in Scotland. The Trust has created a series of nationally and internationally significant arts events, helping to promote the work and livelihoods of creatives including artists, writers and musicians in Scotland.

Most of this work has been achieved through the work of volunteers. Their hard work has paid off and is generating increasing attention from artists, writers, musicians, audiences and press, as well as potential donors and partner organisations.

To mark our 10th anniversary of the Scottish Arts Trust in 2024 and the Scottish Portrait Awards in 2026, the Trust is launching a fundraising initiative. This is our commitment to support accessible, quality arts awards, expanding our inspirational programming to support creatives in Scotland and beyond. The level of prize-money donated and our high-profile judges reflect the growing reputation and good standing of the Trust which have a direct impact on encouraging creatives to take part.

However, this critical funding not only enables high-profile awards to individual and collaborating artists, writers and Young Adult Fiction illustrators, it also underpins the very ecosystem which supports creatives and makes the Scottish Arts Trust so unique. Our support includes exhibitions at Scotland's leading arts venues; digital and online exhibitions; publications including exhibition catalogues, anthologies and new writing; talks and networking opportunities for artists and writers as well as performance opportunities for musicians and composers.

Our goal is for everyone to have the opportunity to showcase creativity. We welcome any contribution to help us on that journey.

Learn more at www.scottishartstrust.org

Printed in Great Britain
by Amazon

57466252R00121